KERRY HADLEY-PRYCE

GAMBLE

CROMER

PUBLISHED BY SALT PUBLISHING 2018

2 4 6 8 10 9 7 5 3 1

Copyright © Kerry Hadley-Pryce 2018

First published in Great Britain in 2018 by
Salt Publishing Ltd
12 Norwich Road, Cromer, Norfolk NR27 0AX United Kingdom

www.saltpublishing.com

Salt Publishing Limited Reg. No. 5293401

A CIP catalogue record for this book is available from the British Library

ISBN 978 1 78463 130 7 (Paperback edition)
ISBN 978 1 78463 131 4 (Electronic edition)

Typeset in Neacademia by Salt Publishing

Printed and bound in Great Britain by Clays Ltd, St Ives plc

Salt Publishing Limited is committed to responsible forest management.
This book is made from Forest Stewardship Council™ certified paper.

GAMBLE

To HIM, SHE'D taste of vanilla, or cucumber, or raw chives, perhaps. She looked like that kind of girl, he thought.

He'll say he'd watched her arrive, and how the van was parked across his driveway. It would have bothered him before, anyone parking across the driveway; that day though, he'd stood at his living room window (the 'lounge', his wife, Carolyn, called it. He hates that word: lounge) and he'd watched her, this girl, through the gap in the mesh of net curtain, and he'd wondered what she'd taste like. He felt a little bit sick - sometimes standing for too long did that to him - but he was trying to ignore all that, and anyway, it was Monday, and he'll say he always felt the cloy of nerves at the start of another week of teaching. So, watching the girl was taking his mind off all that. Words like 'willowy', 'asymmetrical' and 'seemly' mixed with 'uncareful', 'wild' and 'brash' in his mind as he watched her. Her hair, he noticed, was almost blonde - some bits of it were rapeseedy, he decided - and she seemed to have a habit of pushing stray strands behind her ear. She did that a lot, he noticed. He counted. Fourteen times. There seemed a regularity to her way of doing it, and it reminded him of poetry, the way she kept repeating it. She was carrying cardboard boxes into the building opposite and, as he stood watching her, he came to realise he'd never really noticed it, that building. It was a building, and it was just there opposite his 1950s semi. Looking back now, he questions all that. But he was noticing the girl, just then. She wore, he thought, very red lipstick, and that made her look odd, or the lips look odd, like she had a permanent pout, or had been

1

punched, and he found he was forming an opinion about that. He watched her enter the building and then reappear, and became aware that, with every appearance of her, he'd suck in his stomach, straighten his back. Becoming aware of it made him feel somehow ineligible and a little despairing. He'll say he realised then, he needed someone to talk to. Just to talk.

He'd taken to sighing a lot. His wife had mentioned it, picked him up on it, so had his daughter. The two of them had begun, he thought, to behave like a coterie. There had begun to be times where one had finished the other's sentence, or so it had seemed to him. Depressing really. He tried not to think about that, watching this girl. Instead, he tried to guess her age. What would she be? Early twenties? She had enough graceless harmony. Set against the size of the building, she appeared, to him, to enhance the space somehow. The geometry of it made her, or it, look unreal. He'll say she seemed to make the building seem experimental, with absurd angles. Morning shadows, he thought, had created all sorts of distortions. They made the building look very high, for a start, he thought, and made bits of the brickwork glitter like there were sequins, or little pearls, somewhere there. He'd started thinking like this again, thinking poetically. Sometimes, he'll say, he thought it was eating him alive, the poetry. He'd lost touch with his Music Club pals a couple of years back, he'd heard on the grapevine that a couple of them had died of cancer, but he'd started thinking about maybe writing some songs, some lyrics.

In the shower that morning, he'd looked at the muscles of his arm, his biceps, which he could still flex if he clenched his fist. He'd thought that wasn't bad for a fifty-two year old. He'll tell how he removed the plaster a nurse at the hospital had put on the vein in the crook of his arm, had looked at the little rash it had left behind, had thought he must have been allergic. And he'd watched it, the plaster, spiral away down the drain, he'll say he'd wondered if it might eventually cause some sort of blockage he'd have to deal with. He'll say he wanted to cup his hand around his balls, to check, re-check, re-examine, but the thought of doing that made him dizzy, sick. He'd thought, briefly, about the terms 'bloods' and 'biceps'. He'd thought they were odd plurals, a bit of an error perhaps. Now, looking at this girl, this building, though, he did wonder whether there was error in pretty much everything, but he just hadn't noticed before.

A voice from the hallway made him jump, and he realised he'd been holding a mug of tea all the time. Cold by then.

He'll describe how his daughter stood, one hand on her hip. The skirt of her school uniform, he noticed, short, bunched up at the waistband.

'Isabelle, love,' he said. 'That skirt. It's . . .'

He remembers placing his mug down on the arm of a chair, and making chopping motions on his thigh.

'Yeh, yeh,' Isabelle was saying, and she'd begun retreating down the hallway, away from him.

He sighed, thought about moving his mug from the arm of the chair. But it was only a thought. He knew he'd need to move it before he left because he knew, for sure, that Carolyn would be irritated if he didn't.

When he looked out of the window again, he'll tell how the girl and the van were gone, and the lighting had changed, he thought, so the building seemed less big, less pristine, more like a Victorian factory - what had it been? A workhouse that backed onto the canal? The water there is dark and flat, as only that water in Stourbridge Canal can be. He'll say he was thinking, it's alive though, and that's something.

And looking out, just then, he'll say how he realised he could *feel* it, this building with all that girl's things in it, bearing down on him, that's what he'll say. He let it. He let himself identify with it. He breathed it in. He said, or seemed hear himself say, 'Yes.' In the distance, he could hear his daughter's voice saying something about being late, getting into trouble. He felt for his keys in his trouser pocket, his cigarettes, lighter, small change. And he'll say he felt what had become by that time a dull ache, a thump of a pain in his groin. He'll tell how he knew then he'd need someone to talk to at least. He sighed, said, 'I'm there now.'

On his way out, he picked up the pile of exercise books – his weekend marking – from the bookcase in the hall. He'll say how he looked briefly at the way his year nines had written his name: 'Gamble'. Not even 'Mr. Gamble.' He'd sighed, again – he remembers doing it.

The car started on the second go, and he'd turned left onto the dual carriageway, he'll say, before he'd remembered leaving the mug of cold tea on the arm of the chair.

The canal contains lots of things. Things from the past that have sunk right to the bottom and are embedded in the silt and soil and mud, if that's what it is; things that linger in the dark water, suspended, perhaps. Stuck. And the water is greasy with things from the present: oil from Black Country factories, long tall tin cans, cigarette ends, reflections of trees in the shape of people and people's faces. Weeds grow in the canal, yet when they reach the surface, when they appear, when they break through, their death is quick, and their hardened brownish stems poke up and remain still. Only the horizontal image of them moves on the surface of the water, and that only slightly. It's like the air has petrified them, or the water has, and what they could have been has been stolen away.

That day, there'd been a smell. Not the urban smell of dust and smoke. Not the grit and fumes from the ring road. Not just that smell. But a smell of something acidic. No. Not acidic. Something sharp, like pear-drops, maybe. Pear-drops and metal and bone and blood. And sap. The smell that sap makes when it's bleeding from a branch. That sticky, piny smell. As well. Even the rain hadn't washed that smell away.

And there'd been clicks, like the sound of knuckles cracking. Clicks and pops. Childish sounds. Like the sounds you might expect ivy to make, or a twisting vine might make as it grows and burrows its way into walls and round trees; like a tree might make as its branches flex against a weight, maybe; as the bark of the branch of that tree might make as it gives way a little, as it separates from the flesh of the branch, as it squeaks as it bends. Maybe. There were no leaves to rustle, just yet, not on this tree or that day. But had there been, they would have been of the smallish, darkish variety, soon polluted with rain and with dust on the underside.

That day, there'd been an echo of a breath from somewhere, a feel of hair falling across a face and of skin stretching to a break – a tear. There'd been a mouth, open and wordless, and something valuable, lost. And hands with fingers uncurled and heavy.

The school was full of the vocal fry of the young, or immature, or stupid, he'll say. The corridors echoed with it, the stupidity. Gamble was always struck by that. Isabelle was right, they were late. She'd rushed off to class, and Gamble had speculated about how that had changed between them, that rushing off she did. Gone, it seemed, were the days when she'd hug him and tell him to have a good day. The car journey, he noted, was now silent, except for the scratch of noise from her earphones. Did she listen to music? He wondered about that. What exactly did she listen to? Their parting had begun to be instant – it had been that morning. He'd barely parked up and she'd been out, as if to avoid the question of even a word. He'd felt a thought begin to run away with him: she'd be doing her GCSEs in the summer, he'd thought. And then what? What then?

Inside the school, as he set foot inside, he felt as if he'd lost his bearings, just slightly. There followed an acute moment of depression, yes, depression, before he realised exactly where he was – what he was – there. Then, he'll say, he seemed to be suddenly in role, as if the energy that was, essentially, him had begun to leak out, and something else was leaking in. There was all that noise and bother. And stupidity. He'd missed the morning's staff meeting, again, and seemed to be walking – struggling to walk – against the tide of pupils massing in the corridor. He'll say he felt his stomach beginning to churn without really knowing why. He looked at the exercise books he was carrying, at the way his fingers curled round them. Without reason, the fingertips didn't look like his own that day. They looked generically male: square, with the odd hangnail, a bit dirty. But they didn't look like his. He felt a swell of absent vision that seemed to be enlarging as he walked, or moved, more like. And he felt himself tilt, and then the feel of the cold of metal on his shoulder. Was he leaning then? He wondered if he was leaning against one of the lockers. He felt

6

his mouth fill with spit, and from somewhere, a voice, adolescently chinking, saying 'Sir' and then he was somehow sitting, or being sat, on a plastic chair, the back of which strained when he leaned on it. Something, or some things, fell onto the floor, out of his pocket. He'd felt it happen, but his breath was too short, too thin, to concentrate on anything but himself. Christ, he thought, I'm dying. He'd felt like he was a fish, just beneath the surface of cold water, that's what everything seemed to look like, too. Christ, he thought. He might even have said it. Carolyn flashed into his mind, as she is now: heavy around the hips, the chin, with that look that used to be earnest, enticing, and now is just grave. He worked his fingertips across his forehead and felt it like a smear of warm grease. And something seemed to be happening in his neck, his throat, particularly: bubbles, flutters that made him want to cough, and he felt like his heartbeat had reached there and was floundering. 'Jesus,' he heard himself saying. 'I'm dying.'

'You're not dying,' a voice all around his head said, and something, what was it? A paper bag? It was shoved over his mouth.

He smelt his own breath, the metal of it. Carolyn's face retreated, disappointed, as ever, unnatural, black and white, into dead air. He seemed to surface, to come back. And then his mouth was dry. In front of him, when he blinked, when he fluttered back, a collection of interested year eights were being shooed away by the Head Teacher. She seemed to be saying something about getting to lessons, or something about sitting quietly. It was all just a jumble of words to Gamble.

'I'll get to my lessons, Miss Henshaw,' he said, or tried to say, but his tongue was big, dry, like a separate entity.

Miss Henshaw squinted at him. He'll say he saw, he noticed,

7

because she was so close, that she was wearing mascara and he felt an involuntary moment, a flicker of something like want. Either want, or need. He'll say there seemed no-one he could talk to then. It was automatic when he placed his hand on his crotch. The little overhang of flesh above his belt seemed hard, at least, but there was that constant, nagging pain just there. Somebody, some child, somewhere, laughed loudly, he was sure he heard that.

'Go home, Mr. Gamble,' Miss Henshaw said, and it sounded to him like the beginning of an incantation.

Off and away at the back of a thinning crowd, he spotted Isabelle, and the look on her face, it made him feel liquefied.

Miss Henshaw handed him his lighter, some change. She'd picked them up off the floor, had placed them into the palm of his hand, had closed his fingers round them, as if they must have been precious to him. She said, 'Go on, Greg. Just go home.' But, even though he'd wanted to, he heard no kindness in the words.

Gamble didn't argue about going home. There was, is, a heaviness under his eyes; the students, the job, life; they've all done that to him, he thought. His mouth was still dry. He couldn't work out why he was feeling somehow more *diminished*, lately. Less happy, for certain. I should try feeling elated, he thought, I should just tell myself that I'm perfectly fine, really.

In the car, he'll tell how he adjusted the rear-view mirror, caught sight of himself. He'll say that what he was thinking was written in deep lines on his face. He examined his skin like a forensic exercise, stretching it in places with the tips of his fingers. He thought, I'm getting jowly, and something is happening to my mouth. He was thinking, I look like an animal, not a human. He was wondering where his forties went, whether his fifties would disappear as quickly. And that made him feel intensely sad. He saw within his eyes a collaboration of people – his father, mainly, but Isabelle, too – so the sight of himself in the mirror revolted him. He thought it's odd how it's possible to intuit expressions like that, and before starting the engine, he breathed in and out a couple of times, tried to calm, tried to change, literally, but the car smelt of Isabelle's shower gel or perfume or whatever, and it was distracting, and the longer he sat, the quicker the day outside seemed to end. The low light of it dazzled him. It was like some kind of horrible metaphor. In front of him, when he looked, the school, its flat roof, flat car park, flat notedness, became mottled with spits and spots of rain. He shook his head, as if that would cancel the plummeting sensation he was feeling, and swallowed back the notion that life is very short. The very existence of that thought struck him like a thunderclap, but that did not stop it from developing. He tried to rationalise by telling himself he was nearing the end of a hard term, that it would soon be Christmas. Everyone had continued to panic about Ofsted and data and league tables, and most of his students had yawned their way through pretty much all of his lessons. 'Bored,' they'd said, with faces full of spite, unblinking, a terrible confidence about their narrow mouths and eyes.

Christ, he thought. It's killing me. I really am dying.

In the rear view mirror, he caught sight of his jaw, set tight, as he drove away.

Everything had been still. The weather had washed all colour away. Water in the canal had looked like melted wax – like a picture, a photograph. A figure, slim, wearing trousers – jeans, perhaps, a heavy jacket, had stood looking at the water. The reflection, exact, not distorted. The hand, the forefinger of the hand, horizontally across the mouth, the lips. The elbow, held, cupped, by the other hand, tucked right into the body. And down, the feet – smallish – in boots, had made temporary imprints in the mud of the canal towpath. Behind, factories, Victorian – rolling mills, steel stockholders – long-since closed – had stared out with layers of corrugated, half-rusted tin on roofs separated from tall breezeblock walls in places. Glass from the windows was jagged and grey with wetness. A faded paper sign, small, stuck in places, had offered a 'warning to the public', something about authorisation and dangers and trespassing and consequences. And beneath it, and round the corner on a different wall, someone had painted the block outlines of cats, black, standing, sitting, in the process of jumping. Feline silhouettes. Some graffiti by some local art student, most likely. You might say the scene was peaceful. You might. But you'd be wrong.

Across the bridge, in the near distance, a man had walked. Quickly. And as he'd come into view – his head, his neck, his shoulders, his body had come into view – he'd flicked a half-smoked cigarette sideways into the water without looking. And there'd been a hiss. And the figure standing next to the water's edge had seemed to click into motion like a mechanical doll: moving the hand from the face, straightening the jacket. And the look on the face. How to describe it? A lightening of features, eyes widened, a mouth stretched, skin pinkened. From a distance, it had been hard to say. But the man, when he saw the figure waiting, had quickened his step until . . . until he was almost within touching distance. It had been like he'd given himself an enforced moment of inhalation, like he'd wanted to savour that exact second for whatever reason – sometimes you have to allow yourself to – and he'd seemed to be allowing himself to be momentarily vulnerable, and then that's when she'd moved to him, and they'd embraced. No, not embraced, exactly. More hands against shoulders, against arms, against elbows. Cheek against cheek against lips against lips. Shadow noises of movement. To begin with. A pelagic zone of touching. Something and nothing. And then a conversation. Short. Painful. And the intensity of light all around had seemed to change then, become bluer, as if the entire supply of oxygen had been, or was being, used up in the few words they'd been speaking. And their voices had carried along the surface of the water. And the water had been like an unsutured wound.

He'll admit to buying wine instead of painkillers on the way home, from a shop decorated for Christmas. Two bottles. He wasn't much of a drinker, not really. The girl behind the counter, an ex-pupil, asked for proof of age, as if it was the funniest joke.

'You have to look twenty-one, sir,' she said, and her voice was sickly-sweet. 'Or I'll lose my job if I serve you.'

Gamble didn't, quite, recognise her. He'll say, with good reason, it was more than just an occupational hazard, bumping into ex-students. In some ways, it still makes him feel like a minor celebrity, but that's Gamble for you. He'll say he found himself twisting his wedding ring, but looking straight at her. This one, this girl, though, he could tell, would have been a troublesome one. Her hair and nails were blue and she had thick lines of black on her eyelids. In that light, she looked like she was dressed for Halloween. But there was a look in her eyes, he thought, something like adoration, or tease. He instantly fumbled in his bag for his driving licence and then stopped, flushed red from the neck up.

'Oh,' he said. 'I see. It's a joke.'

He tried to laugh, but it came out like a sneeze. It didn't stop him feeling a flicker, though, like he was a teenager, or just a bit younger, again and he'd just heard the name of his secret girlfriend. Of course, he'll say he's just trying to be honest.

Just before he paid, he asked for cigarettes, and when the girl gave them to him, the tips of their fingers touched, and Gamble wondered. He always wondered. In truth, he was weakened, already, then. The girl, he thought, blushed, and gave him a look. How old is she? he thought. He tried to remember what year she'd have left school, but couldn't. She's young, but old enough, she must be, is what he was thinking.

He contemplated asking for something else, the painkillers perhaps, so as to stay there a little longer, but didn't. When he left the shop, he's sure he saw her, through a thick reflection in the window, watching him go. He'll tell how the beginning of a little fantasy involving himself and her flickered into his head. It made him feel daring, sexy, and he'll say he needed that. He felt like loosening the tie, undoing the top button of his shirt, in front of her. He considered going home, getting changed and returning to the shop, just to see if his instincts were right, just to see what might happen. He couldn't help it, Gamble couldn't. He knew he shouldn't think like that, he just couldn't help it, despite everything. But as he walked towards his car, his hands full, the bottles gently knocking against each other, the pack of cigarettes held against his chest, he heard first, then saw a van, white. It was the exhaust, something about it, it was rattling, and it made the engine sound, what, he couldn't find the word, then he did: like a *brute* approaching, he decided. It made him jump, the suddenness of its approach, and his shoes tapped at the pavement like a clock, ticking, or a bomb. They saw each other at the exact same time, Gamble and the girl in the passenger seat. He recognised her, even in that split second. It was the girl's red lips. It was something about the redness of the lips, he thought it was, the kind of pout it gave her. He became aware of the familiarity – not familiarity, more the recollection – of the girl's hair: the colour of rapeseed in places. It was the girl from that morning, the one going in and out of the building. And who was beside her? A thug, by the look of him, Gamble decided, a thug with a baseball cap on sidewards and a grin that wasn't a grin. Even as quickly as the van passed him by, the girl's eyes traced the outline of Gamble's face, or seemed to, then lower, to the pack of cigarettes, the wine he was carrying. The weight of judgment fell like a blade between them, or at least, that was the feeling Gamble had. And it was that feeling that was the decider: he'd drink a bottle of that wine, he thought, maybe both of them, by himself. And anyway, he was just starting to feel the twinge of soreness and slight fever he was getting used to having. Life, he thought, was too short to be disapproved of.

He did not go home. Not straight away. He remembers rain coming fast and heavy, all of a sudden, and the wipers of his car didn't seem to keep up with it, instead smearing water across his vision. He'd opened a bottle of wine as he drove, pleased with himself that he'd accidently chosen screw-top lids. Carolyn, he thought, would be appalled. She'd have been even more appalled to know he'd swigged at the bottle, almost finished it off, as he drove. It had left that taste of vanilla and cucumber lingering on his tongue. He'd tell you, if you asked, that he wanted to feel plucky, carefree. He'd reduce it to that. It's more complicated, obviously. He'd been heading out towards Worcestershire – for no other reason than it's not home – and his head, of course, had become filled with harmonic tension, one sound, one thought, competing with another. Through all of that, he could make out hills in the distance – is it Clee, or Clent? – and there were fragments of lightning, flashing red across the horizon. He could smell the ozone of it, even inside the car, even above the taste of the wine, and that – all of that – seemed to distil into a well of aggressive need. He felt it collecting inside him. Carolyn had always dismissed it, this aspect of him, as his 'freak-out moment', and Gamble had always wondered about that, whether it wasn't simply a tactic, a way of somehow marginalizing him and what he felt. He turned on the radio and fumbled with switches and buttons to find music, but everything he found put different colours in his head and made his chest strain. All it seemed to do was emphasise some emptiness. He had days like this. He'd tell you about them: days when even music – especially music – could not act as a salve or a distraction. Carolyn, he thought, most likely had some theory about that.

He was, momentarily, tempted to drive fast, faster, round the lanes there. For the dare of it. But just the thought seemed to bring on his nervousness, seemed to overlay the fearlessness brought on by the wine. So, he had a tactic he tried to use at moments like this: he tried to take in the 'moment'. He'd overheard one of the Psychology teachers talking about it in the staff room, taking in the 'moment', so he'd tried it, and sometimes it worked, this absorption of the everyday. He tried to take in the feel of the warmth from the heater, the comfort of the seat, the look of the trees, the sound of the rain. He did this and tried to re-calibrate his thoughts by noticing the undulations of the road, and he aligned that with the steady pitch of the engine. The road was thin, little more than a single track in places with a dangerous camber that forced him to hold onto the steering wheel tightly with both hands. Alongside, weather had flattened tall grasses and weeds so that it all looked, to him, just then, defeated. He tried, he really did, to take in the moment, but it was hard and the nervousness, the old anxiety crept back at him. For a fleeting second, he wondered what would happen if he were to close his eyes – how long he could close them for before . . . anything should happen. The thought surprised him, sent a thud through his head, seemed to make him more aware of himself, of the stretch of seatbelt across his chest. It was like he'd woken up from a half-sleep and everything felt like a big surprise, everything looked sharper. And his attention was taken by a field beyond a hedge. The rapeseed flowers had long been cut, but there was still a yellowing that seemed to linger low, and he could see it. And it reminded him of the girl from that morning. Her hair. That brassica yellow. And the slowing raindrops against the windscreen, to him, just then, were like sequins. And thinking of that made him wilt and tense at the same time. And he might remember this next part with more precision than he'd like: he'll say he changed down a gear because there's a bend in the road, a left hand one. He heard water, puddles, *shlush* against the tyres but felt in control,

15

steady. And as he rounded the bend, the grass verge seemed wider, higher. He could see the sandiness of the soil there, made even more jaundiced by the damp, and it made him think of family seaside holidays, ones he and Carolyn and Isabelle had gone on, but only for an instant, because it was then he saw it. It was all in low resolution – wine-soaked, he might think now: a van, white, parked up on the skew on the grass verge, just there. The exhaust, he noticed, hung low, was almost on the floor. And there, standing next to the far hedge away from the road – hawthorn, he thought, the hedge – was a man. He was wearing his baseball cap sidewards this man, and Gamble could make out the existence of an emblem, but not quite what the emblem was on the cap. He could see this man wore a denim jacket, and seemed to be facing the road. He was gesticulating, this man was, jabbing a pointed finger, which made the sleeve of his jacket ride up revealing a line of blue tattooed script – very blue against skin so white it looked palsied. Beside him – no, in front of him, with her back to the road, a girl. *The* girl, Gamble could tell. He could tell by the hair, he just could. As Gamble passed, he was slowed by the corner and the uncanniness of it, the very fact of the look of the scene forced him to try to interpret what was happening. The man's hands, he noticed the skin of them, seemed bright white. There might have been a cigarette between the fingers. Maybe not. It was like he was waiting for something, an answer, maybe, not yet due, or impossible to give. The girl raised her head as Gamble passed, and, as the angle of her changed, he saw her eyes, and her lips. It was like he knew her from somewhere – not just from that morning, not exactly, but knew of her, the *essence* of her. And behind her, that miasma of yellow from the field. He felt something odd in the

16

car, like the beating heart of a frightened child, and heard the bottles of wine, one as good as empty, one full, clink together in the footwell. They didn't break, but instead rolled around dangerously, seductively. Gamble felt the warning of them. There was a moment, a split second, really, when he braked. It was an automatic action, a co-location of thoughts, and as he did, simultaneously, he saw it happen. He saw the man grabbing the girl. He wasn't simply grabbing her, this man, he was grabbing *at* her. Plucking at the air around her, and occasionally catching her, or bits of her clothes or the bare skin of her neck, her face. It was, Gamble thought, as if he was sprinkling something over her. She, meanwhile, stood, rooted, it seemed, but swaying around his touch – a sparring partner, or his property, perhaps. Gamble slowed down, watched it all happening, no, *saw* it, in stark relief, like it, the episode, was being superimposed onto the scenery. He, himself, felt part of the abnormality of it. Look, he thought, look at that. It's the girl from opposite my house. The girl from the building opposite. There seemed, to him, this mix of the familiar with the completely alien. When the man slapped her, this girl, her head lolled to one side – obviously – ethereally, he thought. And when she fell, it seemed as if through a trap door. Gamble felt sick then. He hadn't ever seen anyone being slapped, not in reality he hadn't. He was thinking: did I see that? Really? It was as if he'd thought he'd seen a ghost or a celebrity. Shoddy thinking, he'll say now. He thought he was better than that. That was the kind of thing other people thought. By then, of course, he'd rounded the bend, and when he looked in his rear view mirror, what he saw was the man moving much more quickly, athletically, on the spot. Without knowing why precisely, as soon as Gamble had passed, he sped up, found himself looking for a place to turn, to go back. What for? He was casting himself as a hero, the rescuer. He couldn't just let it go, could he? But the road went on and on and on, it seemed, and the hedgerow closed in, and it felt like a vice. The rain, not so fast by this time, irritated him with its weakness. He couldn't get the wipers to work effectively, slow was too slow and fast was too fast, and they squeaked and vibrated against the windscreen. When the turning came upon him, he almost missed it, trying to fiddle with the way the wipers needed to work, and he swerved the car into in a semi-circle, and he'd begun turning back with really only half a plan. In reality, he was holding back, and he knew it. The way he describes it, the car seemed to misfire, and he pushed the gear stick into first so he and the car together seemed suddenly to rear up and scratch against the wet tarmac. He found himself leaning forward, straining against the seatbelt, gripping the steering wheel so that the bones of his hand looked to be pushing against the skin too hard. He felt like he was holding his breath. The road narrowed, then opened out again, and he knew the bend was approaching and he struggled to look through the raindrops as they fattened again. He pushed the button to open his window, and saw the tint of colour of outside change very slowly. Too slowly, it was annoying. It was more yellowish than he'd thought. If you'd asked him what he'd been thinking just then, he wouldn't have been able to find the words, because words, to someone like Gamble, would have broken the moment, and really, he'll say he was thinking about that palsied flesh and the blue of the tattoo, and wondering, actually, what it might *say*, what the words *were*, scrawled on that flesh, and how strong that slap was, coming from such an inadequate. And he was looking for the girl and the man – the thug – next to the hedgerow. He was looking for them, and even though it had been only moments, and even though – what would he have done exactly? Had a *word* with the bully in the baseball cap? – they weren't there. They'd gone. And the very prediction of looking he'd had, of doing whatever it was he'd thought he might do, melted into a kind of disappointment. No. More than that. Different to that: a relief of disappointment, perhaps. And he didn't know why, not really. And the tension dissolved into exhaustion. And he felt the grip of a tightening band round his chest, then his throat. Both of his hands slid about on the steering wheel and he wiped his palms on his trousers, briskly. Ahead of him, though, he saw it, the van. He could see it as a smear of dirty white. It was disappearing around another bend. There seemed to be an odd camber – odder than before – like driving on a giant football, like the road might erupt, but couldn't, and there was a low vapour rising from the road, or perhaps coming from the van. And the road seemed even narrower as Gamble tried to catch up with the van – not *tried to catch up with* it, exactly, more followed it. As he took the bend, it seemed longer, sharper, the road did, the whole place to him seemed to be acting as an accomplice. And he, Gamble, was leaning in, banking his body, like he was riding a motorbike, or playing a computer game. A trickle of sweat, he felt, dripped down his face and onto his thigh. The wine bottles rolled around in the passenger footwell, still. And Gamble imagined broken glass, spilled blood. He wanted, really wanted, to be a hero. But. But he'll say he was experiencing shortness of breath, a rattle of pain in his neck, his chest, maybe even his arm, the left one, there was definitely a grind of ache in his back, his groin. He became aware of the pitch of his car's engine, and couldn't work out if he was in second or fourth gear. Ahead of him, he could see, way ahead, that is, by then, one single brake light on the van, clearly about to stop at a junction. The vision of grabbing at, plucking and then slapping replayed in double time before his eyes. Except this time, the man, the perpetrator, was not wearing a denim jacket, and he was shirtless, and his biceps were enormous, his tattoos were violent and his spine was burrowed in between mountainous strength. Instinctively, Gamble stopped the car, dead, in the middle of the road. The inertia of it turned his stomach. He watched as the van turned right in the growing distance, back towards the Black Country, at the junction. He was too short-sighted, or perhaps his glasses were too steamed up, or maybe he was too tipsy to be able to read what it said on the side of the van, but he'll say he could make out the motif of a flower, an orchid, like a rude child making a face right at him.

And he felt ridiculous. Or maybe it was hard – impossible – for him to know what to think, actually, or to recognise himself as even human.

He put his hand on his chest, as if to check for a heartbeat. He wanted to put his head between his knees, but there was no chance of that.

The wine bottles appeared from under the passenger seat. They were a goad, on top of everything, they were. Gamble felt himself to be rasping, like there was something at the back of his throat that was maturing. Where, previously, he'd been working off some kind of limbic reaction, now all his thinking seemed over-subscribed – hijacked, even – by threat. He tried to sit perfectly still, but he felt like he'd been confronted with a terrible puzzle, one he had no chance of solving. And when he looked, the far horizon lay strangely flattened, or flattish, except for vaguely womanish inclines that were, to Gamble, undeniable. Factories or high-rise blocks, not quite as far away as Birmingham, hemmed it all in, the entire scene, which, to Gamble, looked so violent at that moment as to be pornographic.

Self-control, he thought. Self-control is crucial. He realised he needed to re-instate logic, reason, before he started losing his presence. This is what he'll say.

It took a while. It really did. He had to pull up on the side of the road. The image of the girl and the man fussed him, as did his own lack of, what? Courage? Manliness? Potency? He'll say he found he was submitting to himself. It was as if he didn't know what he actually was. He felt in his pocket, brought out his pack of cigarettes, his lighter. He let a cigarette hang from the dryness of his bottom lip, flicked at the lighter, which sparked and sparked and sparked, but would not sustain itself. The thought of the girl, and the need to talk, were disappearing, as if downstream, in strangely clear water. He had to use the cigarette lighter in the dashboard of his car. He'd never, up to that point, used that. A first time for everything, he thought. And as he drove towards home, the smoke eased him, but, he'll say now, he was sure he felt malignancy in every breath.

He'll tell how he drove slowly, carefully, this time, without really wanting to reach a destination particularly. The feel of water (not rain, more threatening than that) filled his head, or more like his thoughts, and it was getting dark as he approached Stourbridge. He thought twice about that, going home. And if you asked him, he'd say he doesn't know why he did what he did next, but he must do, really. He must know. He must.

Gamble turned into the cul-de-sac without changing gear – the familiarity of his routine is ingrained in all his actions. He knows this, yet there is no comfort in it, at all, and certainly not that day.

Shaded by conifers on one side, the bricks of his house looked grey, the windows black. It's a family house, symmetrical, clean-looking, with terracotta pots of variegated ivy trailing and evergreens near the door. The lawn looks unkempt, though, and there are weeds growing in the cracks of the crazy paving. Gamble cut the engine and, just for a second, imagined the view he was looking at was the very one Carolyn and he saw when they'd bought the house, moved in, the very view Carolyn had when she'd come back from hospital after having Isabelle. He'll say that day the elevation of the drive made everything seem tilted, made the silence gasp. He pulled on the handbrake, and the car jolted. He sat, as if waiting for permission from someone, somewhere. The still air in the car made his skin prickle and the taste of wine made him regretful. Outside, he noticed, the soil in the borders around the lawn looked greyish – everything did – and he shivered, thinking it was the beginnings of frost, and besides all that . . . besides all that, his head was thrumming with the thought of what he'd seen. He wanted to shift that picture, to shift the worry of it, because it *was* worrying him. It still does.

So, he got out of his car, and he'll say it was a bit like surfacing from a dream, yet, to him, everything still looked as if he was driving past it at thirty or forty miles an hour. He could smell the water, standing there, he thought he could, and as he walked towards the canal, it was like he was above a cloud base. It isn't far from his house, the canal. It's just behind that building opposite. He might have thought going down there, by the water, would have been calm, but, when he was there, all of it had a vividness, like he was making the entire scene up. There were folds of earth that had accumulated and there was, he noticed, thinning in places, stretch marks of a kind from repeated motions in certain bits of the towpath. Just then, it seemed beautiful to him because there seemed a desperate electricity running through that spot, erupting every now and then. Yes, it had *life*. Matted, hardened grass at the elbow of the canal made the flow of water seem sluggish – there are parts that are clogged with the mess put there by others. The weakness can be temporary, hemiplegic, numbed, as if by pins and needles when the electrical or chemical signals sometimes don't work right. Gamble kept walking, kept staring ahead, and it was as if walking there, just then, for him, was intuitive, like a purge. And there was, soon enough, a band of absent vision which enlarged as he walked, inside which he was sure he could see a face, just a face, of the girl.

And there was an assembly of migrating birds. Larger than you'd think. Muscular, but in a vulnerable way, he thought. Whether it was the wine or not, he didn't know, but, to him, the whiteness of them made the sky look corrugated, metallic, almost, bitter. He could feel it, the bitterness. And that landscape, the kick of the canal, the trees hemming it in, he thought seemed to be a reflection of himself. Somehow the sound of his footsteps against the towpath was deadened by something he couldn't quite work out. He was, at first, unsure if it was guilt that was complicating his thinking, or whether it had been – all of it – a hallucination: the girl, the man. Could it have been? He'll say he wondered.

And he had ended up where he'd begun, without realising.

He was outside the back of the building. The girl's building, he realised he'd named it that. The fetch of the wind, it seemed, had shoved him, then had made him start thinking about fate, or, better, destiny. There wasn't even any sign of his usual drinking migraine yet. 'The Flickers' he calls it. And he'll say looking at the building, surveying it, from the towpath, he felt buoyed up, fuelled by something he couldn't describe. He found himself moving towards it, the building, and he was moving differently, he thought, round the side, flattening thick undergrowth. He felt like a hunter, ancient. The light made his shadow look exaggeratedly flat, like an old-fashioned black-and-white villain. He liked that. And he liked the approximateness of the way his shadow fell against the brickwork, the non-discernibility of himself. It was like he belonged to a different race, a different time. All of his reactions as he moved towards the front of the building were, it seemed, recorded against the masonry of the past and he felt unstandardised, unique. He knew, of course, once at the front there, he only had to cast a glance across the road and he'd see his car, parked, on the drive of his house, but he'll say he didn't look. He did not. And anyway, he didn't want anything to hold back the feeling of flowering optimism, if that's what he was feeling.

Maybe it was that, optimism, that made him feel so different, because he was aware that even the process of movement he was using was different from usual. It was as if he was in disguise, and somehow, his courage was a weapon. At the front of the building, the door – he'd never even noticed it before – he'll say now, looked original, Victorian, maybe even older. A beautiful door. Look at the beauty, he thought. Look at it. The curves in the wood, in the panels, were so seductive, teasing, as to be feminine. He looked at it closely. Not at *it* exactly, more at the metaphor of it: something that could let you in and out, yes, of course, but more than that, he looked at the exhibitionist effect, the semantic importance. What he was really looking at was the architect's intention: safeness and the tangible impenetrability it gave to the building. Right at eye level, a plaque, brass, read 'The Old Doll Factory'. He placed his hand, the flat of his palm, against it, that plaque, saw the warped reflection of his life-line, was sure of feeling something like warmth. It seemed, for a moment, unhygienic of him to actually touch it, and when he did, he felt close to tears, especially when it opened, the door. He felt like he had been *allowed*.

Inside, he felt the air travel from him into the hallway. There was, he heard, a definite movement from somewhere, the slap of a curtain or blind, perhaps, that kind of movement. Being inside, having inserted himself there, he'll say he felt strengthened, virile for the first time in, when? He didn't know how long. The inside walls, he noticed, were bare, unplastered, naked brick. There was a shy showiness to that, the pockmarks and imperfections, he thought, that made the inside feel ironically pragmatic, matter of fact. And that, even more ironically, he thought, gave it a softness of structure. But there was a feel of existence in the walls there, he'll say. More than existence - survival. And the floor: tiles, vivid colours, creating a massive geometric shape, looked impenetrable, maybe a little garish and he felt the same, like a protector, irrepressible. And there were, of course, stairs, iron, most likely, or steel. He'll say there was a smell of warm metal on the palm of his hand when he got to the first floor, at any rate.

Because this place was now 'apartments'. And he thought about that word.

He hadn't even seen it happening, this renovation, or restoration, this pulling apart, though he was struck, thunderbolt struck, by a feeling of, not exactly having been there before, but of *knowing* the place, or of knowing *of* it, something of it. The Old Doll Factory. He *must* have known it, he'll say. He'd never lived anywhere else. He'd been born less than three miles down the road. He'd met his wife at the local uni. His daughter had been born in the same hospital as he had. He was nu-Black Country – not working-class any more, but still – this place, it was also 'nu'. He *felt* the place. He *related* to it. There was a connection, for sure. And on that first floor, the impression was of an Ames Room, like he was viewing the corridor up there through a pinhole. Things seemed disproportionate, somehow. The doors, for example, one on either side, there seemed to be something wrong with the perspective of them. They seemed to have been etched into the wall, or out of it. Everything seemed air-tight there.

His mind, his thinking, shifted to the girl moving boxes. The one in the van, the one he saw being slapped like that. The thought was lubricated, warmly, by wine, or heart-burn. Gamble will say he stood there, remembering, no, re-evaluating what he'd seen: the power of the slap itself, the micro-expression on her face of shock, or surprised enjoyment. There was something carnal about that look, something feral. Thinking of that, replaying it, and being there inside that building, he felt a little spark, like the crack of a lighter. Crass to think of it as arousal, more an awakening. He knew if he closed his eyes, he'd imagine, or make himself imagine what it would have felt like to be the one who slapped her. Even with his eyes wide open he could already feel the build-up of strength, the result of a dynamic stretching an athlete does, an irresistibility that becomes itself. What was it that made him feel so bolstered up? He couldn't, or wouldn't, work it out. Just *feeling* it was exquisite and it made him feel balanced on a pinnacle of some kind, arms outstretched, right there, allowing it all to soak in. The formula for a brilliant plan seemed to him to be slotting together in his head. A sort of consummation of everything he'd ever done, everything right, that is: getting all his qualifications, holding down a job. What else? Isabelle, he supposed. He felt himself smiling, at some kind of zenith. It was as if he'd suddenly found an intimacy with himself – no, his self. And the thought of the girl and the security of that building formed a sense of panache he'd forgotten he ever possessed. He knew this breakthrough of consciousness had little to do with the wine, at least, just there in that building, he didn't feel it did. And it was all about feelings then. It was to do with valor, untimidity, but mostly it was about not cracking, it was about surviving. And because it seemed absolutely right – absolutely so – he lit a cigarette. Just lit one, right there, watched the smoke rise up like a phantom, breathed it out, like it was, in fact, part of him, wanting it to stain or impregnate the place. Had there been a mirror, he'd have definitely watched himself, just then.

He didn't stay in there long, Gamble didn't. Just long enough to finish his cigarette, right down to the nub. He didn't knock on any doors, or try to break into any apartments, because, he'll say, he felt reverential, somehow. He even moved more slowly, more precisely, down each step. The act of it had felt like a meditation. He'll say it was only when he emerged from the building, out into the open air, only when he saw

Carolyn's Fiat Panda, heard it clicking to cool behind his car on the drive, did he come round, like he was surfacing from an anaesthetic.

At first, he'll say he thought his key didn't fit into the front door of his own house. Strange, he thought, but there was a flicker of – what was it? – comfort in that, or was it relief? Maybe. But not for long. It seemed like a trick. And he watched himself step inside, catching his reflection in that full-length mirror they have in the hallway there. He didn't seem to look like himself. To him, he was more of a translated version of himself, a photocopy, perhaps, or a photocopy of a photocopy. Not less exactly, just missing some of the worry, with some of the worst bits blurred away. And his own house, the three-bed semi, looked different to him. Inside, the house seemed full of quiet. The hall, when he thought about it, was dark. There was a familiar smell of lavender because of a little wicker basket of pot pourri near the door, but it didn't quite mask the smell of mould or slight damp from somewhere. There is a large candelabra-type light fitting with tear-shaped glass that Gamble always thought looked nasty, cheap, but Carolyn loves. And there is always a box of tissues on a table. To Gamble, the place just felt thick with warning. Even the magnolia walls and bare, stripped floorboards made it feel like life had been removed, or was about to be. There were, he thought, strange, odd-shaped shadows on those floorboards. From where he stood at the front door, Gamble could see the landing, could make out the floral carpet they hadn't replaced since moving in, how many years ago? It had to be fifteen. And seeing the upstairs of his own house seemed to make him feel sick. It was something about being able to see the doors, slightly ajar, of a bedroom or bathroom – a bedroom, especially. Gamble would say the whole effect was exactly like that of a cheapish boarding house, one to escape from in the middle of the night. He'll say he felt disengaged, as if something, or somebody, had plucked everything he'd thought was stabilised in his life, and had moved it, subtly and slightly, to the left, so that it, and he, felt out of whack, sensitised. That was, really, only to be expected.

Maybe it was because his senses had become so finely honed, but he thought he could hear the metal of himself, the meat of himself. For a moment, he felt as though he was looking down on himself as from a viewing gallery: a man, standing on bare floorboards, next to magnolia walls, coats hanging near the door. He looked at them, the coats. There was his waterproof, Carolyn's fleece, and there was a red coat. Isabelle's. The same red, he imagined as the girl's lips – the girl from the building opposite. He smelt it, the coat, the inside of it. Isabelle, it smelt of. But he closed his eyes and imagined the girl.

'What're you doing?'

Carolyn.

She'd changed out of her work clothes and was standing, no, moving down the stairs towards – or maybe *at* – him.

What did she look like to Gamble? A wife? He appraised her as you would a second-hand car. No. She was more an approximation of a wife, he decided. It was the shape of her body, her hair style, the lack of make-up, the shoes. Wifely, yes, conforming to that. Like she'd developed into the role. She had, Gamble thought. She'd got that combative self-importance that only a wife could have, he thought. She'd grown into it, literally, he thought. She'd begun making him feel he had to whisper. He felt like whispering right there, then. She was taking each step slowly in a sort of two-step manoeuvre, as if both her hips and ankles were stiff. She stopped a couple of steps before Gamble, put her hand on her hip, looked at him as if she might be witnessing magic. Gamble watched as she gave that twitch in her shoulders she did when she was incredulous, or half-asleep. She said, 'It's not even one o'clock in the afternoon.'

Gamble looked at his wrist, where a watch ought to have been. He'd stopped wearing one a couple of months before. With his other hand, he still held the material of the red coat, he realised. He let it go, gently. He said something that not even he recognised, in a whisper.

'What?' she said, and she squinted, as if he'd suddenly gone out of focus to her.

'I was just telling you . . .' Gamble said.

Carolyn approached him as if he was a dangerous animal. A snake, he thought. She was glaring at him, at one eye, then the other in that way she tended to, and that always meant something, Gamble knew that and swallowed hard. She said, 'Are you?'

'I came home early,' Gamble said.

'Because?'

Carolyn, he noticed, had had her roots done, but there was something different about that, and he could see the white of her scalp in a more pronounced way. He thought the skin there looked a bit like egg-shell, easy to crack, and he thought about what that might be like, to crack that egg-shell of hers.

'I had a . . .'

'Meeting?' she said.

'No, a . . .'

'A what?'

'Funny turn. A funny turn. A sort of . . .'

'A funny what?'

'Funny. A turn.' He thought about the words. Not really sufficient, he thought.

Carolyn looked him over. 'You've been smoking.'

'It was more of an *attack*. Panic, or something.' That felt better to him, but he needed to be more precise. He wasn't telling Carolyn, really. He was telling himself. He'll say now, he just needed someone to talk to.

'Cigarettes,' she said.

'Anxiety, I mean, is what I felt.' That was better, he thought.

Carolyn was sniffing about him. And he noticed, what he thought was for the first time, lines, fine, like whiskers in the skin above her upper lip. It made her lips look corrugated. A vision of the sky, the migrating birds, from earlier flashed into his mind. She said, 'It's not funny, Greg, it's not good, you smoking like that. It'll affect our insurance.'

Gamble held his breath.

Somewhere nearby – in the kitchen – a clock ticked, and he wondered what she, Carolyn, would look like if he were to slap her.

'Sorry,' he said. It was like a password. He knew the routine.

Carolyn seemed to relax, visibly, but her face remained trained on his. She made a sound that came from the back of her throat.

'Sorry. I am, really,' he said. He was just making sure.

Carolyn turned and walked towards the kitchen. Her backside, in those jeans, Gamble thought, looked flat and wide. When did that happen? He thought, she looks all backside from the rear, and her hair, he could see, it was a different colour: purplish. It's like she's discontented with herself, he thought, like she needs a change.

'Oh,' she said, as if in passing. 'You left a mug on the arm of the chair in the lounge this morning.'

Gamble tutted – he didn't mean to – and she must have heard it and turned to look at him. She was framed in the doorway of the kitchen. Light from behind made her expression indiscernible and her pose seemed somehow constructed. She looked like something William Clutz might have painted, Gamble thought.

'I've left it for you, the mug, for you to move,' she said. 'That is, if you're not too *anxious*.'

Gamble wanted to be obedient. He felt as if he'd been caught red-handed at something without really knowing what. The living room, though, was just as he'd left it. Even the gap in the net curtains. He glanced about. To him, this room had always felt hollow. Like when all the Christmas decorations are removed and it all – this room at any rate – seemed suddenly unfurnished. This room felt like that more than ever then. There were two precisely placed photographs on the sideboard, in between which there was a pottery bowl full of shells. In one photograph, Isabelle. A recent school photograph. Head and shoulders, looking like she was in the midst of saying something, it always seemed to Gamble, her jaw slightly clenched. Something about her eyes, the size of the pupils perhaps, was disconcerting to him. And the other: a wedding photograph of him and Carolyn twenty years ago, more than that. He'll say how he picked it up, how he thought: who exactly is it in this picture? Look at them, he thought. Look at these two people standing so awkwardly, starkly bright – overlit – against a brutalist background. When he looked closely, it seemed that both of these people's feet were hovering slightly above the ground. If this had been a painting, he thought, the artist would have slipped up there. It made it seem like there was an automatic disconnect between the two people in the picture and the exterior world. Even the colour looked artificial, like a sort of mystical apricot. As for Carolyn then, he couldn't see, in that girl there in the picture, anything like the Carolyn now. Then, she was boyish, actually, despite her long hair, he realised, muscular, but in a vulnerable way. He hadn't thought that until then. She looked like someone who needed to protect herself, like someone who could. In the photograph, she stood apart from him, and her dress, he noticed, was crumpled. It was strange, but the gap in the net curtain and the lace on her dress made him think about concealing and revealing. Funny, he thought, how these two people there in the picture, how it all, seemed like a figment of his imagination. And that, he thought, was depressing.

The mug, he noticed, was still balanced on the arm of the chair and he felt something ungood about having left it there, but moving it would have seemed *too* virtuous. He knew he should though, and as he leaned towards it, this mug, he felt a throb of something. It made his breastbone vibrate, his feet itch. It was like the house was trembling. He had to steady himself. And it was as if the room darkened too quickly. Isabelle seemed to be gazing at him from that photograph, about to say something he couldn't, quite, work out. What *was* going on with her eyes? He thought, privately, opaquely, that so much hunger beating at her must be fed from somewhere. He sat, more like fell into, a seated position in the armchair, and the mug fell. Tea, he could see it, cold tea, not much, spilled onto the carpet. And there was a pang of fear then. Through the window, if he'd looked carefully, he'd have seen the white van pulling up outside the building opposite, its engine throbbing. He'd have heard the rattle of the exhaust, seen the driver adjusting his baseball cap so that it rested, oddly, sidewards on his head. As it was, what he saw, what he concentrated on, was not the van at all, but the girl, just her, pulling open the door of the building, glancing briefly out down the road, and going in. And Gamble? He'll say he thought he was dying just then, he really did. That's what he'll say.

The water seems unmoveable, but, of course, there is movement in it. It only seems still. On the surface. But it's like an artery, gently pulsing, keeping things going. Canal water behaves differently from any other type. That surface water with swirls of violet and blue-black and yellow, it seems still, but it isn't. Some people seem to know that. Down there, mud feels like silk under your boots, under your feet, and there's always a smell of warmish sourness in the wind.

'It smells like death,' some people say.

'Don't,' others say. 'Don't say things like that.'

It was the smell, and the lightlessness, and the feel of mud.

Something about the water, though, might make you, *you*, want to plunge your face and hands into it. Might make you want to roll up your sleeves and do that. Might make you want to touch it and let it touch you. Might make you want to break the surface of it and feel movement underneath. Feel the pulsing. Or you might just imagine the gritty feel of it – the dark waters of curiosity – in your hair, in your eyes, in your mouth, in your ears, in your head. Soaking wet with it. Soaking wet. Because it's easy to let curiosity overtake you, isn't it? And a little further up, see the lock – the locks – and see how the depth of water changes. Hear the straining of the weight of it all. It's like it might give way at any moment, isn't it? Even a blind child might work that out.

Isabelle returned from school without her key. Gamble answered the door and his first thought was a familiar rush of irritation with her, but he moved to embrace her as she walked past him, he'll say now, out of routine. It was his usual clumsy attempt and, anyway, she tightened herself away from him. He felt the heavy weight of that and knew he needed to calm it down. From the back, her skirt looked even shorter than it had that morning. She looked willowy, almost like a woman, quite suddenly penetrable, quite suddenly full of promise, he thought, and an influx of something like need overtook him, again. He checked himself, strolled after her into the living room.

'Good day?' he said, and stood, wringing his hands, he realised.

Isabelle was tapping something into her phone, and that amazed him, the way she did that, the speed of it. He'll say he watched her for a couple of seconds. She sat, no, she flopped, in that way that she had, down onto the sofa. He wanted to tell her to sit gently, but knew he'd say it to her with a bright, over-bright, voice, and didn't want to. Instead, he looked at the photographs again, and the pottery container full of shells. He walked over, picked up a shell. He'll say now, he just wanted to *communicate* with her, that was all.

'Do you remember when . . .' he said.

Isabelle crossed her legs. He could see almost to the top of her thigh. There was a ladder in her tights, he noticed. She said, 'Oh God. Dad. Not the "do you remember" thing.' It was not her voice she was using. Whose was it?

'No, Isabelle,' Gamble said, and he was turning the shell over in his hand. 'Listen. Do you remember that time when . . .'

'No. I don't. I don't want to.' She was looking at him like she was the parent.

'What?' Gamble said. 'What's the . . .'

'Nothing,' she said. 'Leave it.'

She sighed, and he saw the beginnings of corrugations above her upper lip. No, he thought, surely not.

'I was just going to say . . .' He put the shell back. He sounded like a newsreader, he thought.

'Oh, God. Dad. Just. Don't.' She put her hand across her eyes as if she'd seen something grotesque. She even hesitated before she said the next part: 'I hate it. I *hate* it when you're "just going to say".'

But Gamble, he'll say now, he wasn't picking up on the cues. He should have left it there. He should have read the signs and gone up to the spare room there and then, but he didn't. He said, 'I was only going to say about that time when you were little and we were . . .'

Isabelle moved as if she'd been electrocuted. She stood up, and her phone dropped onto the floor. She held the top of her head with both hands, her eyes were her mother's.

'Yes, yes. The time on the beach. The shells. Yes. Blah, blah. Let's. Not.'

'Isabelle.' His tone was wheedling and he stepped towards her. Poor me, he was thinking, what's up with her? But she moved away – dodged away – started, he thought, looking through the gap in the curtains.

'Never mind about when I was a little girl, what about today?' she said.

He wanted to hold her, calm her down. He used to know how to. But he was flummoxed. When she turned round to face him, he saw what she'd look like when she was thirty, or forty.

'Do you know how . . .' – she sniffed around the room for the word – *'embarrassing* you are?'

She lisped it. He knew she did that, lisped, when she was tired, but just then, the look of her, to him, the look of her teeth, the very tip of her tongue, when she spoke made her look like some kind of creature he couldn't quite place.

'Embarrassing?' he said.

'You *humiliated* me,' she said. 'The way you looked at Miss Henshaw this morning. It's *humiliating.*'

She was speaking as if she'd just learned the word 'humiliating'. She nurtured it. Saying it seemed to fluff her up, Gamble realised, like a bird, like one about to migrate.

'Do you know what you *look* like?' She'd become all fluff, all limbs, all arms. Gamble had to step back and she'd stepped forward. It was like some kind of salsa.

'You look *sad.*'

'Isabelle, love,' he said, all placating, all fatherly. 'Where's all this coming from?'

And it was like she'd been jolted again. Crass to say she flew at him. But she did. Her upper body seemed separate from the rest of her, her arms at an acute angle behind her. She was like a diver in mid-air, but all face and voice, coming towards him.

'Probably trying to impress her with talk about your *writing.* Your *poems* you can't get published?' She was sneering. She looked inhuman. 'Don't think I don't know what you're like.'

'What I'm . . . ?' The exchange was going too fast for him now. To him, she seemed to be speaking as if she was texting. If he hadn't been so confused, he'd have been amazed.

'You and that . . .' She paused, wrinkled her nose. It was her mother's face again. 'That *girl* from before. *Hannah*. You impressed her, didn't you?'

Gamble's thoughts began jig-sawing into place, and she must have seen it happening.

'Yeh,' she said, and she was nodding slowly, an actor, a detective now. 'From before. When I was *little*. I know all about it. Mum told me about that little *affair*. You like the *ladies*, don't you, Dad?'

He said, 'Isabelle.' Because it was all he could muster and it was all in this minor-key voice he didn't quite recognise was his. He wanted to say, he wanted to tell her that was a long time ago, something like that, but the banality of the phrase stopped him, and anyway, Carolyn's shadow flickered across the hallway. He felt himself straighten his back like he'd put himself on alert. Isabelle was saying something about doing what she wanted.

'I wouldn't ever hurt you.' He heard himself saying it just as Carolyn came into view. 'I wouldn't,' he said, and he was aware he was looking at Carolyn. He was taken by the expression on her face. What was it? He couldn't work it out. Unsympathetic, for one, mixed with something close to gratification, or was it hope?

'Bollocks.' Isabelle. Was she swearing now? And crying?

Gamble stepped towards her, wanted to say something, but kept hitting dead-ends. 'I don't . . . I didn't . . . I mean, you shouldn't . . . Just come here . . .'

'Oh, shut up, Dad.' She was flapping her arms, birdlike. Her nose was red, her neck. He hadn't realised it was possible to feel so hammered with spite as he did then, and he stood, wringing his hands, running his thumb over his knuckles like they were sore.

'What's happening to you? What's happened?' he said. He whispered it, actually, as if it was something just between the two of them.

Isabelle snatched at her school bag, swung it onto her back (Gamble thought, what *does* she keep in there? Why is it always so full of things?). He said, 'I'm worried about you.'

And quite suddenly, it seemed there were razors in the air, and everything was happening in slow motion. Then Isabelle said, 'Just . . . drop dead . . . just . . . fuck off.' And the way she said it, it was like she was the one in charge. And then she just walked away from him. She sauntered, more like, is what he'll say. As if moving like that was an art she had perfected. It amazed him, that, the way she moved. And she sort of shimmied past Carolyn, and it was as if they were in perfect synchronicity with each other, those two. She shimmied past Carolyn and faded herself away up the stairs.

He felt all worked up and calmed down at the same time. It was like there was a baseline thudding through him he ought to have been able to control, but couldn't. He could feel his heart beating in his neck, and was sure Carolyn must surely be able to feel it, too. The silence she was creating made him yearn for a fast chaos. Was this what falling off a cliff felt like? He imagined it must be. The only inevitability being the pain at the end.

Carolyn was motionless, but for that twitch, the shoulders. Not really even a movement, he thought, more like a

39

suggestion. Her mouth had narrowed though. Gamble saw that about her. He sighed.

'Well done, Greg,' she said, eventually, and when she climbed the stairs, she didn't look back.

Later, awake, alone in the spare room and smoking cigarette after cigarette, he was sedate. He was thinking about things from the past, embedded but dug up. And about things from the future, possible things. He watched the day end in a fading slice on the far wall. There might have been the smell of water, slightly bitter, from somewhere, the smell of raw chives. And that would have made him think. Even in the half-light, he could make out the bruise on the crook of his arm, and the rash and the little pinprick. He examined the way the vein stood out there, like a wire under his flesh. He'll say he thought, am I frightened, or frustrated, is that what it is? Am I frustrated, again? I might be, savagely so, and he recalled the image of Hannah, briefly, but shook that away. That was too solid an image, too real. It was the thought of the girl from the building opposite, the way she might look, the way the eyes might look at him, the set of the face, the lips, the slightness of the body, he concentrated on. The way she would need him, listen to him perhaps. The way he could protect her, keep her safe, the way he could talk to her. The way she would make him feel like a man again. And he stretched to embrace it. There'd be a glisten about the eyes, he thought, like pearls. Her inadequacy, the fact of her, suddenly strong – implanted – in his imagination, and he was bolstered by the sense that he was waiting for something not yet due. Not. Yet. To him, it was a certainty though. And a sweetness as intimate as water filled him and seemed to even out a scrimmage of, what, desire? Yes, probably.

When things are as good as dead, it doesn't matter about colours or smells or such things. It just doesn't. Because the light and the air are full of tricks in that snap of time. And that's the thing about the water. People think canals are full of stagnant water, but they aren't. It isn't. It isn't stagnant, the water. Far from it. It's alive, watchful. But only just. Only just alive. If there's sunlight there, it has no warmth in it. It's just as good as dead. And there's a type of person who frequents that sort of place. They're the ones with the blind expressions, pale. On anyone else, it might move you to tears, but this look they have, as they stand by the water's edge, it might make you angry because, actually, they are bare-faced with lies. Think of that.

And those footsteps, they were quick, down by the canal. They were quick. They were light. Feet, bare, rain-wet, mud-wet, slipping in the sludge.

There's something about Black Country pubs that isn't like pubs elsewhere. There's a diligence about the way they've been kept, as if the removal of sawdust, say, or the redecoration of walls would be heresy. They like to think of themselves as 'real' pubs, vacuums from a past time. Gamble had been thinking about this as he'd sat in a corner of one. This was four years back and he'd been writing poetry, lots of it, at the time. He'll say all sorts of metaphors seemed to keep springing into his mind. It had been flowing out of him and he'd been spending a lot of time in the spare room on the computer, typing it all up. He'll say he was on his second pint and the other men had been talking about Brian Eno, and he'd never even heard of him, so he'd settled himself against the fixed seating, wishing the time away, he'll say. He'll tell how he'd only gone to Music Club because Carolyn had suggested it.

'Get an interest, for God's sake, will you?' she'd said. 'I wish you'd just get an interest.'

Which is, he'll say, how he'd met Hannah.

He'd worn a shirt, denim, with his jeans, he'll say now, but the others seemed to wear a uniform of T-shirts with various bands' names on – most of which he didn't know. Mostly, he'd kept his shirt buttoned up and his arms folded. At least, he'd thought, there's beer.

He'll say he'd already decided he'd never come to another of these meetings, no matter what Carolyn said. He'd thought being there, being surrounded by men like that, was like being in a fishbowl. So, when Hannah had walked in, he'd noticed her straight away. He'll say he'd noticed something about her, something familiar.

The rest of them were talking about Loudon Wainwright and he'd felt a surge of middle age that he knew he couldn't bear. Christ, he'd thought even then, is this what I am now?

And he'd noticed she was looking for somewhere to sit. She'd been wearing a blue dress – new, as Gamble found out later. What he'd noticed about her was the way she moved. He'll tell how she had this light way of walking, like there might be a trip-wire she'd catch herself on if she wasn't careful. She'd positioned herself on a high stool next to the bar and the strap of her dress kept dropping off her shoulder so she kept energetically slipping it back into place. It was that about her, that movement, and the look of her legs – runner's legs, he later discovered – that caught Gamble. That, and the white of her skin – very white, he'd thought. He'll say it was fascinating to him.

Someone, he heard, had said 'One man guy' and without really thinking, he'd stood up, straightened his shirt, pulled in his stomach a bit. He said, 'It's my round, guys.'

Of course, he was braver then. Remember, this was four years ago, or thereabouts. He was more muscular, darker, a bit. He'll admit that he slipped off his wedding ring, put it in his pocket.

She'd turned, half-turned, as he approached the bar. He'd leaned against it right next to her. The point of her knee grazed his thigh. Without looking at her he'd said, 'Hey, let me get you a drink.' He said it like a recitation, as if everything was a foregone conclusion. Talking about it now, there's a hint of embarrassment in his voice.

He'd felt her, sensed her, observing him, and for a second, as he leant on the bar next to her, holding a twenty pound note, he'd thought she was about to slap him. But she'd said, 'Just a tonic water.' And then, 'No, put a gin in it.'

He'd nodded and smiled. It might have been relief. She was a local, he could tell by the tight vowels, but there was something else, something more familiar than that. Out of the corner of his eye, he'd seen her place her handbag on her lap, and her dress had ridden up. They were, both of them, playing a part just then, he realised – or he realises now: him, cool, but sufficiently interested. Her, poised, in waiting. It had seemed important to him not to actually look at her. He'd wanted her to wonder why he didn't pay her more attention, so he'd watched the barman select ice cubes from a silver bucket, keeping his back turned. There was that thud of excitement, or potential excitement going on between them, though, Gamble and this girl, he could already feel it, or at least, this is what he'll say now.

She leaned forward, said, 'Actually, no gin.' And that had made him turn to her. She'd said, 'Change of heart.'

And he'd liked that. He'd thought it ept. So they were there, the two of them, just looking at each other.

'Sorry,' she said, 'I'm a bit . . .' and she moved her hands in a circular movement. Red fingernails, of course.

The barman had placed the drinks on the bar, and Gamble slid hers towards her, and with it, himself. She was older than he'd have preferred, he thought then, but there was a thin silver ring, pierced, through her lower lip and he'd focused on it.

'Cheers,' he'd said, and, when she'd replied, she'd clicked at the ring with her tongue, like she'd been rolling ideas round on it and Gamble had liked that. He'd liked everything about her all in one go just then.

He was appraising her, Gamble was, and he'll tell how it seemed to make her feel fuller, more patient, and she altered her position, seeming to know the strap of her dress would slip, just a little. He liked that. She twisted her body, placed her hands on the bar to steady herself. Gamble knew it felt sticky, the bar did, but she left her hands right there. She seemed to know that doing so stretched the material of her dress, and she seemed to know he'd be looking. Small pleasures, he thought, and it was he – it was him, Gamble – who reached across and slipped the strap of her dress back into place, and he'd watched her face as he did. And she'd let him do it. She'd allowed it. The skin of her shoulder wasn't as warm as he'd thought it would be. A second, a moment, wavered when he thought they might have a conversation, that she might turn and lean across to him. She did not. Not just then. Instead, she watched him. She breathed, he thought, or will say now, as if desperate, or as if preparing to say something. She breathed at him, it seemed, and looked at him like he might accuse her of something at any moment. He heard – they both would have, surely – music, piped music from somewhere, a melody, something familiar. More people entered the place: another group of men, maybe four or five of them, wearing suits, their ties loosened. They brought with them a Friday night relief, and air, and the sort of low hum of chat that vibrates around certain places at certain times. She, Hannah – because that's who it was – became watchful. It was a subtle change, for sure, but he could see it in her. The men crowded the bar, jostled Gamble. They're playing the part of businessmen at play, he thought. They ordered whisky, loudly. They laughed, but not really. Gamble remembers one of the men noticed Hannah, nodded at her. It was an appreciative nod, Gamble thought, and felt instantly – and without any right, he knew – possessive of her. She seemed to pretend she hadn't seen that and sipped her drink. The ice in her glass splintered and cracked. Gamble heard it, heard her swallow, saw her look away. She crossed her legs, uncrossed them – it seemed to be a habit she had, he noticed, like she couldn't make up her mind – and he noticed the points of her knees, and he thought, then, she was probably the most beautiful thing. He perceived her as such, then, that is. The song, the music, came to an end, and another, a softer one, began. It felt like a theme tune for the moment. The men ordered more whisky, and she'd glanced over at them only once. One of them, Gamble thought, was still looking at her, squinting at her. Around them, the cadence of the men's talk seemed to alter. Gamble had one hand in his pocket, the other was holding his drink. He was leaning against the bar, wanting to look, what? Casual? He lifted his chin as he looked at her. Now he thinks about it, there was a menace about her he didn't, quite, get. Not then.

In fact, it was just before she spoke that he realised.

'It's you,' she said. 'Mr. Gamble, isn't it?'

She pronounced his name oddly. He couldn't tell whether it was a slur or just a strange discomfort. Either way, he'll say now, it made her – her voice, the way she spoke – even more interesting to him.

She seemed to slip herself off the stool, to step towards him like someone about to swat a fly, and dipped her face towards his, and she smelt him – smelt *at* him: his aftershave, powdery by then, he'd imagined. And he should have known, then.

'I know you,' she said, and she was very close to him, her skin almost on his. 'You taught me. To write.'

She moved the upper part of her body closer to his face. It was like an dance technique, he thought, that movement. It surprised him how graceful the movement was: the way the legs were, the hips, the opening of the arm and clenching of the hand. She was, he thought, like a ballerina holding a hammer. That was the poet in him at the time, thinking things like that. Her eyes, he noticed, flared. She looked reckless. The rest of the men turned to see. The way the lighting was, he noticed, gave her a glow. He'd been trying to place her in his past.

'You, Mr. Gamble, taught me to write,' she said, and she paused dramatically, holding an invisible pen in her hand. It's deliberate, this pause, Gamble had thought, because she must be able to see that she has everyone's attention. She leaned heavily against him, leaned her chest against his arm, and, it seemed, either fell or placed her clenched hand on his thigh, very slowly splaying her fingers on his leg just there. 'You taught me to write poetry, at secondary school. You were great. My favourite.'

The men in suits - Gamble remembers this - seemed to be mesmerised.

'You don't remember me though,' she said. It was a statement.

She's squeezing my thigh, Gamble thought, and when he looked, he could see her knuckles silvering. It felt more than intimate.

'I do,' he said, but very quietly. He'll admit that was a lie, now.

Somebody, the barman, perhaps, said something, but he didn't hear exactly what because another song had started and the steady beat of it seemed to be vibrating through him. She said, into his ear, 'Hannah. I'm Hannah.' And it was an echo of a breath from somewhere else, and he felt her hair skimming his face. Her eyes were bright wet and she'd looked at him like she was counting money, and for a moment, he'll say he was scared she might do something rash, like kiss him there and then. He had an uncomfortable feeling of delivering himself into an unknown, and he'll tell you he became acutely, beautifully, aware of his surroundings, just then: the irrationality of the pattern on the carpet; the strange angles where legs met table tops; the open fire. He became shockingly aware of all that. The light, magnified, it seemed, made it look like the blue of her dress was melting, or perhaps changing its state. Raindrops, or snow, or just her skin, glittered like sequins across her shoulders. To him, it was the stuff of photographs. He could only see the woman in her face, not the schoolgirl - he didn't want to see that, anyway. And across her mouth, her lips, he saw a terrible confidence. He tried to imagine how that happened, that confidence.

'You don't remember me,' she said. 'Not really.'

Gamble cleared his throat. His voice seemed low to him.

'I'm quite a . . . disappointing man,' he said.

How had he wanted to seem? He'd immediately wanted to take it back. He put his hand in his pocket. It had looked casual, but he'd been feeling for his wedding ring, checking it was safe.

Her mood seemed to suddenly change, she seemed, to him, to become anxious, aggravated, and though he was sure he could still feel her grip on his thigh, when he looked, she'd moved her hand and seemed to be staggering back, or losing interest, he couldn't work out which. She did what she did next automatically, really, it seemed to him: she seemed to slide off and away, walking backwards at first. The strap of her dress fell, again, and she'd seemed to let it. Looking at her move like that, Gamble had felt like he was leaning, banking, to the left; he felt as if he'd had too much to drink, but he knew he hadn't even had two pints yet. And, he watched her leave, and she wasn't even particularly quick.

Gamble woke up coughing. His first thought was of Isabelle and what she'd said, how she'd said it. He'd scratched at his arm where the bloods had been taken and it was sore, the skin there. He'll say he'd dreamt of Hannah for the first time in three, four years, but he'll say now, it was probably because of what Isabelle had said. How did she know about that? So it was a surprise to him that he'd slept at all, and the first waking sensation was the smell of smoke, still sagging about. It made him want a cigarette. He couldn't see the point of giving up

48

then – or now – but the pack on the side was empty, so he'd sat up, had examined the crushed-out stubs in the ashtray, had found one that was still smokeable and had lit it, had lay back down. This was the spare room he was in. He'd thought it best, he'll say. In the corner of the room, on a desk, his computer, out of date, for sure, now, he thought, and leaning against the wall, there was his old guitar (without his spectacles, and through the smoke, he could make out the shape of a woman in the body of it. He let his gaze linger there for a bit). There were cardboard boxes, box files, half-empty bookshelves, a couple of shirts hanging up on the outside of an old wardrobe. He'd sweated overnight, and the duvet was stuck to him. When he moved it, shoved it away and off him, the skin of his chest, his belly, looked like kneaded clay. There was a sticky, piny smell coming from him. It reminded him of something, someone, and that made his mind drift. He thought, I should be feeling something here, I should be feeling lonely, or sad. Here I am, he thought, in this single bed. I'm alone. I'm amongst the spare parts. But, he just didn't feel any of that. Instead, he felt like he was in the midst of an experience. He lay still and felt bolted to the spot, not even properly human. He looked down on himself, watched his chest rise and fall. I am a man, he had to tell himself – he told himself – I *am* a man. I am a *man*. It was a mantra, it had become one.

He'll tell how night-time had become a problem for him for him. Night-time had been when the darkness closed in and the terrors had tightened. That's how he'll say it felt. He'll say it'd been like he felt his own heartbeat, had heard it in his head. And it'd felt and had sounded irregular, like it'd been about to stop. Like he'd been about to be punished. He'll say, in the old days, he used to hold Carolyn, and he'd let her

49

put her head on his chest out of routine, but he'd turn onto his side when her breathing had evened out and he'd thought she'd fallen asleep. He wanted to tell her he'd come to dread it, night-time, to say how he'd felt shattered, on the edge of sleep a lot in the day, but at night, how he lay, dreading it. It'd been his dreams, and then the dread of waking up – the act of waking up – to another day. He'd hated the quiet of night. He'll admit he realised he hated the need to relax, because he thought he knew what happens – or what could happen – if you relaxed, or if you take your eye off things, if you'd trusted, say, fate, or someone else. And he hated the start of another day. The hope of it. The false hope of it. Pills help less now than they used to, he'll say. So, he has begun dealing with it in his own way. He smokes more, drinks, but only sometimes. And sometimes he'll say he'll just sit, quietly, in the kitchen or in the spare room. Just sit there. And, to him, it is as if he's broken. Like he's been two people: the bright bloke, sometimes making cheeky jokes, a bit crass, a bit Jack the Lad, but stiff-upper-lip, taking it all in his stride, apparently reliable husband at least. And then there's this terrified, unhappy man, crying in toilets, going through the motions; yes, going through the motions but scared, angry, needy. And he's done a good job of leading this broken, double life of his because he wanted people to think he was coping – he wants them to think he's coping now. And Carolyn? It's like he's been confused by a mix of temptation and disgust for her, even in the early stages. Sometimes she'd look at him and that's what he'd think. And he thinks, she's broken, too. I've broken her. And we're both lost.

He's right, in a way, you can get lost, you can lose yourself, even in small towns, even in the Black Country – especially there, you can lose yourself. Time is different there. Gamble knows this. He'll say now, time is different for him now, and he just needs someone to talk to.

And if you ask him, he'll tell you. He'll say how he's not been a bad person. Not a bad man. Not really. But he believes that bad things have happened to him. And he believes that isn't fair.

And so he lay there, naked, in the spare room, cooling from his own heat, the cigarette having burnt down to the filter and having gone out, but still held between his fingers. There was a slice of daylight, razor sharp and still, on the wall opposite. Words like 'willowy', 'symmetrical' and 'seemly' mixed with 'uncareful', 'wild' and 'brash' in his mind, and he was sure he could taste vanilla, or raw onions – something like it – at the back of his throat. He let his fingers stray down his chest, down his belly, and he thought – he said aloud – 'I am a man. I am.' There was a heavy ache, just there, just then. And when he felt further down, he could feel it, this ache, as clear as ever.

Ask him about Hannah, and he'll say her breath had smelt, and tasted, of pear drops.

He'd gone after her, Gamble had. He'd gone after Hannah. He'd felt like a hunter, leaving the pub, leaving the drinks on the bar, the Music Club men. It had been the combination of everything: the voice, the way she'd moved, her face, that dress, the strap, everything. She'd seemed to have been willing him to follow her.

And leaving the pub had been like leaving a vacuum. The outside air had rushed at him – strange air, he'll say now. His stomach had lurched with it. What was it? Hunger? In a moment of panic, he'd thought she'd disappeared, or had driven off – he didn't know whether she'd driven there. The glare from the car park lights seemed like an insult; better, like a protection, an enforced pause, trying to prevent him from seeing. But he did see her. She was little more than an after-image, a negative image. It might have been the sound of her heels clicking against the tarmac that he heard first. And he'd called her name, but the wind had been against him, had blown it back into his face. He was fitter then. When he thinks back (he tries not to) he'll say he remembers racing after her, although, most likely, it was more like a jog. There'd been the urban smell of dust, smoke, all that, in the thickness of the rain, but there always is in the Black Country. It wasn't so much that. It was him, the way he was behaving. He felt prototypical, driven by something he didn't understand or want to understand, just then. He caught up with her at the canal towpath. It was gravel then, that first part, near where the narrowboats could moor, and she'd glanced behind at the sound of him. She must have been able to see he didn't know what to say. He'll say she looked contrite, and stood still. Rain had stuck her dress to her body, her thighs, her stomach. As far as he was concerned, she might as well have been naked. Her hair had flattened against her head, her face, and she looked thinner, is what Gamble remembers. He would say he felt deferential, coy. He ran his fingers through his hair, realised he'd left his coat behind in the pub. He'd wanted to laugh, at himself, for being ridiculous, for even thinking . . . but he was there now, in front of her.

'I wanted to . . .' He was going to lie, but changed his mind, knowing it would sound stupid, and she'd see right through it, anyway, of course she would. But she didn't move, or speak. It occurred to him that she seemed to like what was happening, or what could be happening, and she held out her hand.

Rain fell hard against her face, and, it seemed to him, she'd lifted her head up to catch it in her eyes, but she didn't even blink. She seemed spellbound, locked onto him, he thought. When he took her fingers, the very tips of them, her grip surprised him. She curled her hand round his, and pulled him to her. It made his knuckles crack. Behind him, further back, far back, the hum and hiss of cars on the ring road made him feel like he'd stepped out of society, that he'd become, somehow, an original, and when he walked, when he followed her, he was like a toddler, like he'd regressed into another life, walking into the dark.

He remembers the look of the canal, though: greasy, green-ish black in that light. The air was just as strange down there, and trees stood like orphans, waiting. He kept walking, trust-ing her. To the side, past the old house, there's the weir. If you get off the towpath there, you go into the woods. They did, those two. There'd been clicks and pops as they'd walked across the understory there: fallen branches, sticks and so on. He was struck by the beauty and danger of the smell of wet wood. It smelt, to him, like blood. But there was shelter there. The trees sheltered them, despite the lack of leaves. He remembers her stopping. He remembers standing with her, his chest against her back, and feeling her head lean back against him. Just then, he felt like he was hovering between life and death. When she turned, she said something he didn't catch: a question, he could tell by the intonation. Did she say something about being careful?

'It's alright,' he said. 'It's okay.'

He'll tell how he might have sounded charming, or cajoling.

Either way, it seemed to soothe her, and, anyway, he'd made it sound like fate had overtaken them both.

And then she'd turned and seemed to be leaning her back against a tree. What was it? An oak tree? A willow? He felt he should have known. He placed the palm of one hand on it, next to her ear. Rain had saturated the bark, and it felt like sponge, but it didn't matter. He skimmed the flesh of her there. Soft. It felt like it, like everything, was *giving*, saying, 'Yes, go ahead.' There was less than a flickering half-light there, and that made it painfully exciting for him, at the time, the way that only sometimes could he make out her features. Only sometimes could he see how she was concentrating, on him. She could, he thought, have been anyone. He'll say he'd never done anything like this before. Not even with Carolyn. Especially not with her. This was not his self, there, he'll say. It wasn't *him*. And he was working things out by feel with his free hand. He was feeling his way around her. What sounds? Branches flexing – he guessed she must have been gripping branches; the sound of bark giving way, separating from the flesh of the rest of it; her feet, the weight of her through the movement of her feet, positioning, re-positioning herself, a little unstable, perhaps; her breath, catching, a lovely reluctance about it, seeming to echo; the feel, the sound of skin stretching to a break or a tear; of hair, falling across a face; the smell of soil – she must, or he must, have been disturbing the earth beneath their feet. Her shoulders, he saw the skin of them shimmer, the shadow in the crook of her neck near her collar bone. He wanted to eat the flesh there, he wanted to bite into that part of her. He licked it, just there, like a dog might, and he felt her mouth, open and wordless against him. She tasted of – what? Something acidic. Her hair, the smell of it.

He didn't want to lose this feeling, this feeling of power that seemed to be building in him. He felt one of her legs, like a twisting vine, seeming to grow, to burrow its way round him. His teeth felt big in his mouth, and he could taste his own spit on the flesh of her shoulder. When he bit her just there, she didn't make a sound, but she tensed, as if shot, and the movement was quick, she had his face in her hands then and she pressed her mouth on his. Not so much kissing as biting. He didn't know whose blood he was tasting. And that ring through her lip, crunching against his teeth, he could taste the metal of it, of her, and he felt, automatically, for his wedding ring, still in his pocket.

Later, at home, Carolyn was already in bed, the nightlight was on in Isabelle's room, the house was almost deadly silent, except for their breathing. His reflection, his face, wasn't his. The eyes looked like they'd seen an apparition, or a spell had been cast on them. He'd snatched a couple of tissues from the box they always keep in the hallway there and had wiped his mouth. Upstairs, he ran cold water and soaked Isabelle's Disney flannel, dabbed his face with it. He glanced around the bathroom at all the female paraphernalia there: Carolyn's various essential oils, candles, Isabelle's bath toys. Jesus, he thought, I'm surrounded. Strangled. There'd been mud on his jeans, and when he'd looked, there were footprints in the hallway, up the stairs. He moved, sat, quite suddenly on the top step. He couldn't, quite, get his breath. He'd run home without stopping – but he must have been fitter then. He could smell himself, or her – Hannah, that is – on him. Something sticky, piny. When he ran his hand through his hair, there were fragments of wood – twigs – and a wet leaf there. A button was missing off his shirt. There was blood on his T-shirt. And his lips . . . his lips were a mess, he could feel them swelling by the second. Even his hands felt heavy, bloated, difficult to uncurl. And so he ached, literally, and metaphorically. Because he hadn't thought he was that type of man. Yet when he sat there, and he could hear his wife and his daughter breathing – echoes of breath – and even hearing that, even though it reminded him of Hannah, her breath all over him, he didn't feel guilty. That wasn't what he'd felt. He'll tell how he'd felt like a man *should* feel: like he'd been in a battle, but was satiated now, was victorious.

He'll say he hasn't talked about this for such a long time, hadn't realised how much he needed to.

Gamble tends to tell you things as he remembers them, but out of order, out of time. Sometimes it's hard to keep up or work out if he's talking about things that are happening now, or a few years ago. But he will say about how, recently, in the spare room, having slept there, he grabbed one of the shirts that was hanging up on the outside of the old wardrobe, and used it to wipe his face, his armpits, his chest and stomach. He didn't want to shower – that would wake Carolyn, for sure. The other shirt, the denim one, he slipped on. He hadn't worn that shirt in ages. Years. Now, of course, it's a little loose. He fastened it, disappointed about the missing button. There is a full-length mirror there. He'll say he thought he looked a bit tired, a bit weathered, and there were prickles of glitter along his jawline, but not bad, he thought, for fifty-two. And a sonnet – Shakespeare – flashed into his mind. He'd probably remember the lines properly if he sat and thought, instead though he'll say he thought about growing a beard, the economics of it as well as the way it might make him feel. Shaving had always been craft, to him. He was a master at it, and he enjoys doing it – he's that kind of man. He enjoys the procedural effect of it: water, soap, the method of actually shaving, the shape, the stretching of the skin, then more water. And the smoothness of the face afterwards, the generally smooth effect. And maybe, sometimes, the feel of the aftershave. The brutality of it. To him, it's manly, that, the brutality, it's part of the process of being a man, he thinks. So, there, in that spare room, he'll tell how he examined his face closely. The beard, he realised, would be grey, or greyish. He wasn't so sure about that. He pulled the skin around his jawline. It is basically a good jawline. Not bad, he thought then. He considered his posture and straightened his back. He'll say he noticed how much weight he'd lost, but it was early – not even seven yet – and the light wasn't good in that room. The early hour gave him the urge to go for a walk, maybe a run, like he used to. He wondered if he'd still have the energy. Actually though, he wanted a cigarette, and maybe to sit in one of the cafés in town, just to people-watch. There was something about the temperature of him, he thought, standing there, looking at himself like that. He considered he was basically tepid by nature, but at that moment, he could feel something boiling up, surging up. He'll say he felt European, bohemian, almost optimistic. He'll say he thought, I might not take my painkillers today, or maybe I'll take half a dose. And he thought maybe he'd start writing again. He wondered if what he could feel was poetry, again. He realised the need to be in some kind of flow, and he looked at the computer, at the dust on it. There were hundreds of his poems saved somewhere in there, and the start of a novel, of course. And he thought about all that, the novel, the poetry.

Through the window, when he pulled the curtain, the sky

was a growing purple, changing as he looked at it, as if it had been slapped – thumped, perhaps – and then told off. He could see the building opposite from a different perspective, of course, and he stood for a while, looking at it, fingering the empty buttonhole on his shirt. He hadn't realised there were chimneys, four, on that building across from him, or balconies. The brickwork of them looked beaten up, weathered, but not in the way he looked weathered, they looked more artful, he thought, more designed for effect. He could see the way the bricks had flaked away, or had been made to look flaked away, whereas he, well, he was, is, the archetype of weathered, the result of a gradual and inevitable deterioration. He touched his face again, just as the radiators started to click. He'd grow a beard, he decided, there and then. And he'd write some poetry. Thinking that felt like a revelation, just then. So it was perfect – more than perfect – when he saw a light in a window – dim, but still – pretty much exactly opposite, in the building, but the venetian blind was closed. He put his spectacles on and was sure he could see a silhouette passing across the slats. He willed them to tilt, the slats. The figure, he could see the outline, was struggling with something. He kept willing, hoping, it was with the mechanism, the – what is it? – thing you have to turn or pull to move the slats. He had the impression whoever it was – the girl, he hoped – was confused. He was straining to see, but he'd started to sweat. He thought it was his proximity to the radiator, and wiped his forehead with his sleeve. When he moved to one side, he could see the postman walking towards his house, and it distracted him, the thought that he might be seen gawping out of the window and he felt ashamed, briefly, but when he looked again, the blind in the window had been raised completely and he could see the girl. She was there. That she was there and alive, what did he feel? Relief? Yes, that, certainly. He watched her move about. She was just, he thought, going about her business. She was the epitome of that. And, God, she looked so *young*. She wasn't naked, but almost. The underwear was flesh coloured, the same colour as Carolyn wore, and that surprised him, but the skin, even from where he was, was different and he could feel his own fascination with it. It was as if she wasn't old enough to have eaten enough to have gained any spare weight. She wasn't slender, so much as skinny. Underweight. Bones, he saw, in places he didn't realise he should be able to, especially from a distance. More than that, the way she moved, this girl, like she was on wheels, or, no, more like she flowed, like she was in water, or she *was* water. Odd, to him, that way she had of moving, but not moving. And what did he feel about this tightrope of voyeurism he knew he was walking? Actually, he thought at first, she looks like fair game, moving about like that, with the blind raised, she might as well have been completely naked, or have walked out onto the balcony and waved at him. But that she was unsuspecting, unaware, was the thing. Just that glimpse of her. He imagined himself there with her. He let himself imagine it. Even though it made him feel instantly lonely, discontented with what he had, what he'd ended up with, he wanted to keep watching her, he wanted to hold the image in his head then, as if he could make her into something precious, as if by doing so it would act as a salve for his thoughts about her, about himself. If he thought of her as you would do a gemstone, say, or an Old Master, then it would be alright, acceptable to photograph her – mentally that is – to imprint her on his memory so that he could revisit the image, or summon her whenever he wanted. He was already convincing himself that doing so would, amongst other things, keep her safe. This was why he didn't try to look away, just yet, in case she disappeared, the way inspiration or youth, or friendships, or love can disappear. And then he hated himself for even thinking it. He stood further to one side, out of view of the postman, he hoped, and thought briefly about clichés: how generally clichéd this whole situation was. There he was, a middle-aged man watching a near-naked girl, but feeling a load of worry lift away from him that she was safe, unharmed. That was one level, the paternal level. But he couldn't, quite, let go of another feeling. The poet in him thought, '*My glass shall not persuade me I am old, So long as youth and thou are of one date.*' What was the rest? He couldn't remember. Something about death and something about beauty, and something about the '*raiment of my heart*'.

Even thinking the words made the hairs on his arms, on his chest, stand up – Shakespeare always did – and when he looked again, she, the girl, had disappeared from view, and he could hear post dropping on the floor downstairs, and even that sound seemed mellow to him then.

He'll say he found his old trainers under the bed, blew dust and cobwebs off them. God, he hadn't worn them since, well, for years. The sole of one of them was cracked horizontally along the tread. He examined that. There was old mud and gravel caked there, and before he put them on, there were bits of twigs he needed to empty out onto the carpet. Wearing them again made him feel something. What was it? Less tight, urbane. They made him walk differently.

There were scraps of paper on the desk next to his comput-er, a notebook and a pencil. He picked them up and walked out onto the landing. His bedroom – his and Carolyn's, that is – was at the far end. He had to walk past it, to creep past it. He could hear soft snoring through the closed door. And he felt a surge of something. Kindness, perhaps, or something in the raiment of his heart. But it was coloured by the image of the girl from opposite and knowing she was safe and she was *there*, in the Old Doll Factory. It seemed important to him that there was someone else there, someone other than a wife, he'll say, a *possibility*, for him. He can't explain it precisely, or doesn't want to.

Downstairs, there on the mat, one letter, the emblem of the NHS in red. Bending down to pick it up, he glimpsed the name 'Gamble', and it was one of those moments where he felt that it wasn't his name. He saw it as if it was an alien word, not even a name at all, in fact, more a statement, an actual act, as if everything he was that was bound up in that name no longer was. It was a deliberate disengagement, he is capable of that. He folded the letter, unopened, and shoved it into the back pocket of his jeans. Later, he thought, I'll have a look at that later. And he left the house quietly.

When Gamble wants to talk about four years ago, he'll say he remembers it all well. Four years. Odd to even think it now, he'll say. And he'll say how she'd made him feel irrepressible, Hannah had, irrepressible and impenetrable. At first, when he'd thought about her, when he'd thought back to that time near the canal, he'd felt this kind of warm lubricant flood him. He'll say that afterwards, he'd prepare himself to think about her, almost as a meditation – and this was before he'd heard of the 'moment' and living in it – and he'd picture her, or he'd picture a version of her, then he'd edit, and then edit a little more. He'd close his eyes to be able to see her, in his head, more clearly, so that he'd be able to concentrate, so that he'd be able to flitter from one point of interest on her body to another. She'd seemed infinitely more attractive that way. The thought affected him, it reverberated – she reverberated – around him, inside him. He was still writing poetry then, and sat at his desk-top, tapping away, and he was reading poetry, too: Aphra Behn's wandering thoughts and untamed hearts made him feel as if something had been unlocked, like a door, or a passageway back to his youth, or perhaps forward to a libertine future. There were moments, four years ago, when he felt euphoric, as if he was dragging everyone – Carolyn, Isabelle, his work colleagues, his students – along in his wake, as if he had become irresistible. Words came to him, and like water, they flowed through him with absolutely no effort. Often, the only problem was that he couldn't keep up with them, the words. It was as if they were running away with him, as if he was floating, just a little, above them, and everyone else's life around him was somehow inferior, or maybe not inferior, maybe just more abbreviated. He made jokes in the staff room at work, he sang in the shower, he spoke to the neighbours, he did silly magic tricks to impress Isabelle, it didn't bother him when students chatted or hadn't done their homework. He developed an interest – a desire, he thought – to know how things worked: remote control, WiFi, satellite TV. Odd scientific things. He became conscious of his posture, his facial muscles even. He had his hair styled. Styled, into that modern mullet that was fashionable back then. He grew a beard, and then thoroughly enjoyed the act of shaving it off. In the back of his mind, he had the entire plot of a novel, just waiting to be written. He could hear things, hear them clearly, that he hadn't heard before: shadow beats in music, under-voices in choruses of songs. At night, he could hear the canal like it had some kind of life, some kind of flow that he had only found by listening very carefully. He thought he'd found a kind of groove, that he was so sharpened – mentally and physically – that he'd be able to run a marathon or solve equations, or both. Back then, even Carolyn said, 'What's happened to you lately? It's like you're on drugs or something.'

He'd even laughed at that because he'd felt a wave of kindness towards her for even noticing. Kindness, yes. And warmth.

And he'd thought, at the time, it was because of Hannah, because of having had her.

And he'd thought this was the start of something better. He'd been more patient of Carolyn's moods, of her pickiness, of the sense of disapproval she sometimes gave off, even then. He'd *understood* her more, he'd thought. He *got* her. She works hard, he thought, harder than I do. Something to do with science, she worked in, something to do with research at the local university. He wasn't absolutely certain what it was she actually did, and felt guilty for not having ever taken an interest. Look what she's ended up with, he thought: me. Poor Carolyn. He wondered, without asking her, what kind of man she'd wanted him to be, what she'd expected of him. He'll say that in truth, when they'd met at university, it had been her ability to remain calm, the sense that she was, in fact, 'wife material' that had been the attraction. Thinking that, then, made him feel arrogant, and a little ashamed, but it was true. He'd chosen her, he knew – he had *chosen* her – because the thought of being with someone who might *depend* on him sent him running for a metaphorical bus. She, Carolyn, was never going to do that. The others – and there'd been plenty before her – would, he just knew, have called on his resources too much. Carolyn, though, was the opposite of needy. But. But, and he knew this would happen, practicalities inevitably began to outweigh emotion, he thought, or romance, or desire. By which he meant they lived – they had developed into – this orderly life. Professionals, both of them. Middle class Black Country people, doing okay. Underneath though, underneath, he'd had this well, or pit, of fire that he seemed to be constantly having to dampen down. Carolyn either never noticed, or stopped noticing, or ignored. He'll say how he watched her gain weight. The chins, the belly, the thighs. He'd watched her expand, whilst her interest in him, the connection with him (if that's what it had ever been) contracted. He'd watched her eyes glaze over when he'd tried to talk to her about his poetry, or his students, or music, or films. And it had been a gradual, almost mutually agreed, parting of selves, he'd felt, with her forging forward with her career, being a mother and so on. He'd looked at her sometimes as they sat watching TV, he'd watched the way her jaw dropped very slightly, and the inside of her mouth became visible, and, yes, he'd felt utter discontent. At night, he'd felt the heat from her and had started shuffling to the edge of the bed. Often, anyway, she'd been fast off before he'd even brushed his teeth. More often than not, he'd cruised through the TV channels and had ended up falling asleep downstairs, or in the spare room. Then, Hannah. Hannah had changed everything. She had recalibrated him. She'd made him see things differently. When he thought about it, in simple terms, that fire, the one he had, up to that point, kept under control, had blazed down there by the canal, with her. Once he'd got through the wonder, the shame (yes), the fascination, the gratitude, he felt renewed, as a man. And, of course, he'd thought he'd got away with it.

Of course, he'd avoided going to his music nights after that, instead, telling Carolyn that he was working on some writing. Which was true, he was. And he'd felt as if the machinery of his life had been oiled and was working well. He seemed to be able to see his situation, his home life, more clearly. Poor Carolyn. He'd felt sorry for her. He'd felt this kindness had actually materialised. She worked so hard.

He'll tell how she said to him one Saturday – it must have been 2013 – 'Have you ever thought of cleaning the shower after you've used it?' She was holding a sponge, a container of cleaning fluid. She'd appeared at the door of the spare room where he was working, where he was writing, and had walked round behind him. Her neck was a mass of red blotches she only ever got when she was some kind of excited, and he could see more of it, her neck, then because that was the first time she'd had her hair cut short. He made himself feel kind. He gave her an apologetic smile, said, 'Sorry, love. I am a bit hopeless.'

'Yes, well,' she said, and left the words there, but her shoulders were twitching.

'Tell you what,' he said, and he was only just thinking this as he was saying it. 'Why don't we get a cleaner or something?'

He realised, even then, that they were in performance, the two of them. They were performing a marriage – what they thought a marriage should look like. They were modelling it primarily for Isabelle: that was Gamble's reasoning, at least. If she could see how it should be done, even if they were improvising, making up the words, then he'd have done his job. He thought then about telling Carolyn he loved her, but didn't. Instead, he said, 'Hey, look. I'm going to write a novel.' He pointed at his computer screen, was nodding at it. Carolyn stood so that she blocked out the light from the window almost completely. He thought then, Gamble did, it's not so much the silence she creates, as the patch of time before I know she's going to say something. To him, it was like some kind of dark fog he had to get through. He saw her shoulders twitch, again. She said, 'I'll sort a cleaner out, after I've cleaned the shower, prepared dinner and collected Isabelle from Brownies, shall I?' And she left.

He'll tell how he thought, I'll never want her again, Carolyn. Not like that. He didn't know if he'd miss it, miss her. He didn't want to predict. He thought, then, I'll never leave her though, because I have to *care* for her, and for Isabelle. It was because he didn't want Isabelle to have come from one of those families who can't do it properly, he'll say. Isabelle was the thing. And anyway, he thought, at the time, he could manage himself, that there might even be more Hannahs. And he thought it was easy to keep secrets.

He heard her, Carolyn, twenty minutes, maybe half an hour later, still scrubbing away in the bathroom, and tried not to feel irritated.

Two figures had stood, one of them naked, or as good as, on the towpath, looking at the water, looking at its swirls of thick colour. The water had seemed unmoveable, glowing almost. Still. Both of them had seemed to know that place would outlive them. Of all the people who walked here – who still walk here now – these two had given at least some signs of appreciation of its beauty, or its age, or something. When the breeze skimmed the water there, when the cold froze it, when the scabs and blood and secrets were quiet and hidden there, most people didn't see or feel it. Didn't see or feel any of it. But these two, they did. And it's true, it takes a certain state of mind to allow that type of thinking, because it was always dark down there at night – even before night - and you could get lost in that blackness. And these two figures had started to walk into that blackness, and it was as if they'd been walking on nothing into nothing. Because sometimes the darkness down there, it can make you think you're blind, as if you can't be sure if you're alive or dead yet.

But both had seemed to know.

Because it takes a certain state of mind to allow that kind of thinking.

And they had stood on the towpath, one of them naked as sin, as good as, and the water had seemed still until one of them had spat noiselessly into it.

Hannah had tracked him down. He'll say that's how he felt about it. That was his first thought. About her. She'd asked the men at the pub, the ones in the Music Club. She'd been there every Friday, for weeks – for more than a month. Eventually, and she told him this, she'd followed him home from work, from school. And she'd waited for him just round the side there, at the bottom of his road. Seeing her, he'd felt, as soon as he'd seen her, besieged. He'd thought he'd stored her as just a memory. To him, standing there, like a gatekeeper at the bottom of the road, she'd looked like a different kind of real. She'd looked wayward. And he'd jumped on the brakes, had felt his thoughts scramble. He'd wound his window down. It had been getting on for springtime and the smell of laundry drying on lines should have seemed wonderful, but didn't. It felt ridiculous. She didn't move from her spot on the pavement, and he crept the car forwards, pulled up beside her. Her clothes, he noticed, were contrary to her age, not in fashion, as if she was pretending to be someone else, or, he hoped, was trying to be inconspicuous. His house is on a slight incline. He could see it from where he was and it looked, to him, faultless, precious even. He said, 'Get in.' And then, 'Please.'

He'll tell how she didn't move particularly quickly, it was like she was still on that tightrope, and that seemed to make something start to flood through him. When she sat next to him, he couldn't seem to drive away quickly enough and thought it made him seem foolish.

After a moment, she said, 'Where are we going?' And he said, 'Away from here.' And the fact that she'd said 'we' like that had grated on him.

This is what he'll say: that he drove out, he didn't know where he was heading. The fact of her sitting in his car, where Isabelle, where Carolyn had sat, made him feel something: queasy, or immoral somehow. The tone of the engine, the way it was screaming through the gears, seemed to epitomise what was going on in his head. On the back seat, his notebook, where he'd scrawled poetry during his free period at school, slid about. Just then it seemed stupid, bizarre, for it to be there. Without realising it, he seemed to be driving out on the dual carriageway. It had only been minutes, he was sure. There was a cluster of ideas he was having: something about driving into Birmingham; something about a pub; something about dumping her in the middle of nowhere. But she said something. Her voice had a mellow sternness. It was a low hum.

'What?' he said.

'Stop, Greg,' she said. 'Just stop.'

It was like someone – she – had stuck a pin into the situation. Like she had located something, and things had just deflated, or relaxed.

Gamble pulled into a layby, like he was obeying her. He cut the engine. All he could hear was his own breathing. There was a whistle coming from his nose that he couldn't seem to stop, like he might be sickening for something, a cold perhaps. But he could smell her, he could smell her hair. It was like she hadn't washed it. It was that kind of smell. And he could smell the smoke on her. Vehicles were going past in the carriageway next to them too fast – fifty or sixty miles an hour, it seemed – and his car rocked gently with every passing one. She, though, she was all calm. White with it. He said, 'Look. That, before, it wasn't me. That wasn't me. I don't do things like that.'

'Sshh,' she said. 'Don't say anything.'

Light from somewhere glittered in her eyes. He could feel them, her eyes, all over him. There was that menace about her, right there, and he saw it. She was concentrating – she is concentrating on me, he thought – and that made him feel like he was spreading, mushrooming into something, someone, different, despite himself.

She said, 'Greg,' like it was the start of something tragic she had to tell him.

'Oh God,' he said. 'Oh, God.' And he let his forehead drop down onto the steering wheel. He was thinking: baby. She's having one. She can't. It'd be mine. I'm already a father. I can't go through all that – all this – again, or at all.

But she put, she *rested*, her hand on his leg.

'Sshh,' she said. 'I just wanted you to know it's all okay.'

He looked at her then, properly, for the first time. Being in the car there, with her, like that, with cars and lorries advancing and receding, it was difficult to feel stationary. She said, 'It's okay. Really. Relax.'

He saw then, or he'll say he saw that she was wearing the same clothes as she'd worn before, or something very similar, though there was something different about the way he saw that. He knew, if he looked, he'd be able to see the shape of her body through the material of her clothes. And he tried not to. She, though, she really was concentrating on him, and that made him feel, what? Objectified, he'll say. She crossed her legs, and he glanced at the point of her knees. Something beautiful about the way she did it made him want to forget how he should be feeling.

'I only wanted to say I know you're married,' she said, and she moved her hand away from his leg. 'And . . .' She was looking, gesturing towards the glint of his wedding ring and it seemed automatic that he'd twist it, with his thumb, like it was no secret.

He wanted to kiss her, then. He wanted to taste her again. Fleetingly, he wondered what was wrong with him, why he thought any of that.

'And, well, I didn't want you to feel, you know, *bad.*' She uncrossed, then crossed her legs again. 'Not *bad,*' she said, and she'd started to sound irritated. 'Not that. I mean not *guilty.*'

She wasn't wearing any make-up, he noticed that. Not like before. She looked older, a little tired. She said, 'I wanted it to be clear between us. You know? I mean . . .'

He wanted to feel her breath, it was something to do with proximity, something to do with the air inside his car, and the movement of things, and where they were in that layby, and that dip in the skin between her neck and her collar bone, and he said, 'What's wrong with me?' and he was

70

talking about his feelings, about how he knew he ought to be feeling.

'Nothing,' she said. 'Nothing at all. You're lovely. You are. It's just . . .'

Just what? he thought, but only fleetingly, and he didn't say it.

She said, 'I mean, I can't . . . I wanted you to know, you know, in person, that I can't, you know, do that again.'

Her voice had taken on that caramelly quality she'd had at the pub. He didn't know, quite, what she meant. The car was full of cross-purposes. She wasn't looking at him any more. She was all voice to him then. There's no baby after all, then, is what he was thinking. It might have been relief that was mapping its way through him. But there were also stories. Stories that were rolling around in his head. And poetry.

'Jesus,' he said. It was partly relief. And he caught sight of his notebook. He leaned across to the back seat, and noticed she, Hannah, didn't move, like she might have been expecting something. He felt, with the notebook in his hands, quite suddenly full of something. Panache, perhaps, or relief, more like. He wanted to show what he was, that he was, perhaps, some kind of creative athlete. He flipped open the cover and tore out a page of his poetry. In his hand, though, the paper, the ink looked insubstantial - really - freshly torn like that and he said, 'Sorry' and he passed it to her, like an offering.

'Oh,' she said. 'Thanks.'

He saw that her fingernails were bitten, that there were nubs of flesh on the fingertips as she took the paper from him. He said, 'It's not Shakespeare or Behn, or anything, but, you know . . .' He wanted to appear kind, smart. It was, really, the relief.

She said, 'What is it?' And he said, 'It's a poem. I wrote it. It's just a poem.' And he felt for a second he might have to define what he meant. But he saw her lips start moving, and heard the whisper of her voice. It was an old poem of his, not a very good one, really, he'll say. He watched her read it through.

When she'd finished, she said, 'Wow,' and she was pointing to a line on the paper. She said, '*One surrealist woman holding in her arms the skin of an audience.*'

He'll say, even now, he felt himself blush. She said, 'Interesting.' And he thought how thin it was of her to say that, how feeble of her.

'Thanks,' he said. And there seemed nothing else he could think of to say, either.

There was a pause, not even worthy of a comma, before she folded the paper into four, and he wondered, just for a second if she'd throw it away once she was out of sight.

She moved, a little uncomfortably, he thought. The folded paper looked fragile in her hand. She said, 'So, anyway, that's it, really. Your wife – Carolyn, is it? – I won't say anything to her. Or Isabelle, is it? Is that her name? I won't *say* anything.' She smoothed down the material of her skirt along her thighs. 'Just wanted you to know that, you know, in person. I just, I mean, I just didn't want things to, you know . . .' and she seemed to be waving the air or the words away from her.

He's cagey about saying it, but up to that point, he'd wanted her. He'd wanted *her*. But he did nothing, especially not after she'd said Isabelle's name. Hearing that from her had withered him. He'd felt himself wither. He said, 'How did you . . . ?' And she'd shifted in the seat there, told him she'd followed him from school and had happened to see or hear Carolyn call to Isabelle outside their house. It was all vague.

He'll say he started the car. His fingers were trembling. She'd followed him from school? He couldn't stop thinking about that. He dropped her off in Lye, she'd asked him to. She said, 'It's all okay, Greg. It is. It's best to end it, it is, really.' And her skirt rode up so he could see the smooth of her thigh as she got out of the car. Before she closed the door, she said, 'And thanks. For this.' And she waved the folded paper about her head like she was bidding for something. Gamble heard himself swallow, watched her break into a run, just like she was escaping from him. He drove off towards home quite fast – it was like they were escaping from each other, he'll say – but had to park up as soon as he thought he was out of sight. He had to park up in a side street and sit quietly for a few minutes. He was shaking. He'll say he felt all his thoughts hardening off, and filling with ideas about conspiracy, looking for things she'd said, but hadn't said, things she'd said but really what she'd meant. He'll say he was thinking he'd taught her to write, that, yes, she'd said she wouldn't *say* anything. But, he'd taught her to *write*. And that made him shake.

Back home, he'd ended up sitting by himself in the kitchen. He'd shouted at Isabelle as soon as he'd got home. Carolyn was lying down with a migraine. She'd started getting them regularly then. He thought it wasn't so much a migraine as an eruption of disappointment, in him, specifically. He'll say now that he'd rather she'd have got angry, fully, properly furious. But she seemed to channel it all, all that disappointment, in him, into stuff that could only come out as a migraine. She was blinded by them, he knew.

'Mum's got one of her heads,' Isabelle had said. She was writing something in a notepad in the kitchen. What was she then? Eleven years old? Ten? She liked writing; the act of

73

handwriting, she seemed to like it then. When Gamble looked, she was writing her name over and over again. Seeing her do that made him feel unsteady.

'How do you spell your name, Dad?' she said. And it was innocent. An innocent question. He told her, or thought he had. He spelt it out. He was talking, he realised, in an automatic way. He was thinking about Carolyn upstairs and how inconvenient her migraines were becoming, he was still thinking about what to do about Hannah, what she might have meant. When he looked, Isabelle was carefully writing 'H a n n a' because those were the letters he'd given her. So he'd shouted. At her. Made her cross it out, tear the page out. And he'd ended up sitting by himself in the kitchen, rolling thoughts around in his head. And Isabelle was in her room.

This letter he received from the hospital, he didn't open it. Instead, he'll say he folded it, unopened, and shoved it into the back pocket of his jeans. He'll say now, of course, that he knew it was the results of his blood test. He'll say he thought, I'll have a look at that later. And he left the house quietly. The Old Doll Factory, he stopped and looked at - more than that, he looked into it, again. He'd stood there on the narrow pavement and he remembers rubbing his wedding ring and the skin round it just there, and he looked into it, that building, into the fabric of it. He saw his breath in weak lines, and heard that whistling noise he sometimes makes when he's ill or sickening for a cold. If he'd have looked behind him, he knows now that he'd have seen Isabelle at her bedroom window, trying to get some natural light so she could put eyeliner on. There wasn't much of it, natural light, in her room, because of it being blocked out by the building opposite. He'd have seen her step behind the curtain, out of his sight. But he wasn't looking that way, he was looking up at a window in the Old Doll Factory, at the tilted venetian blinds, beyond the balcony there, trying to look into it, trying to see the girl in there. There was blurry point of light from somewhere in there, more haze than light, like it came from a computer or a naked flame and that made him try to imagine what kind of place it was, her flat, what kind of place she, the girl lived in. Something about bottles of wine and packs of cigarettes, something about sentimental knick-knacks and photographs in fancy frames crossed his mind, and music. There'd be music. James Brown, Marvin Gaye (or would that just be too obvious?). And he looked at the glow, imagined it was, in fact, light from a screen, that she would be working at it, tapping away, like all young people did, living a virtual life, perhaps. All this, he was thinking, imagining, before he realised he was staring. He was willing her to appear, and he felt bad about that, it felt crude, creepy. None of that thinking seemed to be his style. He thought he knew what his style was. He thought he had a fair amount of insight by then. He prided himself on that.

But he did want to think about her. He'll say now, maybe it was in a fatherly way, in a caring way, out of concern for her – for what he'd seen happen to her. He wanted to have her in his thoughts. He couldn't, quite, put his finger on exactly why he wanted to do this. Dangerous ground, he knew, but, see, Gamble was, amongst other things, bored, and lonely, and he knew it. And that's a crazy combination. He knew that, too. At least, that's what he'll say now.

He'll say he could smell the canal, and that made him want to smoke, and he lit a cigarette as he walked across onto the towpath. The smoke was gorgeous to him, it helped him think. It cleared his head, actually. It had been, what, four years since Hannah, and right then, he'll say he realised he wanted someone, yes, but he wanted someone who would make him read between the lines, someone even more damaged than him who would make him feel or know something about himself he didn't already. A closed curtain, maybe. He felt the urgency of that. And there, just then, he yearned for the fall, for something more than just desire. He wanted to plummet the depths, not paddle the shallows with rolled-up trouser legs. He wanted more than that, more than just skin was what he wanted. And, of course, he was thinking about the girl. He was imagining tapping at her door, imagining the way he'd tap at that door, not loudly, not urgently; there'd be no need for that. He was imagining the smell of her skin, her breath, the clumsiness, the platitudes, and the disgust. He thought about the disgust he ought to feel afterwards, but only briefly. He imagined all that. And his footsteps on the towpath, there, scratched gravel against mud and he heard, no, he was *aware* of his own receding paces, as if he was walking away from himself. And he was surprised at the relief he was feeling. It was like some kind of disciplined rapture, like something celebratory. For a moment, he closed his eyes, tried to imagine what she would look like close to. There'd be something about the eyes, something nervous, slightly reluctant – only very slightly – or something you could interpret as trying to be superior, or just careless. He'll say he couldn't quite decide on what colour her eyes would be – blue or green or silver, the colour of water. And there'd be a swell there, more like an ocean. When he opened his eyes he was casting a shadow ahead of himself. His shadow-body looked long, and darkness rippled and bowed outwards like something trying to get out of him. He was thinking, look at the shape the hands are making, the cigarette there between the fingers. He watched the slope of the shoulders and the shape of the neck, the chin when the head turned. And he watched the shadow and the canal repeating itself. Repeating itself. He thought back properly, for the first time in a long time, to Hannah as he walked. He didn't feel the same as he had done then. Not at all. He was a different person then. He remembered – he made himself remember. He thought, all these years and I've tried not to even think of it, of then, of her, but she's always been there, hovering in the background. He thought back to nights he didn't sleep. He remembered standing, sitting, standing in the bedroom, watching Carolyn, hearing her body moving about now and then, being aware of the vibrations in her throat, and wishing, really *wishing* he wanted her. He remembered the view from the window, the hills hardening from whiskery beginnings. Clent, he was pretty sure. And beneath them, the housing estates, uneven and as hard asleep as Carolyn was. He remembered how he'd felt a hunger or a need because, when he thought about it, Hannah had proved something. Not proved, perhaps, had stirred something, in him. Having had her, that is, the fact of that: that he was still alive with it, that he was still a man, is what he thought. And that thought flickered into something lovely sometimes. He remembered watching the sun seep into the edges of things, and feeling this thin twine stretching between him and that life he had there with Carolyn, and with Isabelle. There were shells, then, a couple, that Isabelle had collected the summer before, had presented to him, and he'd kept them on his bedside table. She'd seemed to love him, then, for leaving them there so he could see them when he woke up. He thought, yes, she loved

77

me then. But she, Isabelle, had made him feel like a *father*, and he hadn't been sure about that, had he? Worse than that, she'd made him feel like a bad father. Sometimes, the thought of that had left him weak, or weakened, so much so that he'd had to sit down, or go to the spare room, sit at the computer, stare at the screen and wait for poetry to come to him. But he was still with Carolyn, and he'd watched Isabelle begin to grow up and away from him. And he thought about that, and how his relationship with Isabelle had a system, like the weather: sometimes it rose and cooled, it formed clouds or it was in depression. There could be anticyclones of high pressure, and sunny, warm times between them. But it was all so unpredictable, and he couldn't keep up with it. He realises that now. Being a father, the feeling of being a father, to him, it is like a grief. And he needed to carry it around with him. He needed not to forget it. So, he became it, physically. It lifted him and it dragged him down. Sometimes it energised him, and sometimes it drained every single thing from him.

Beside him, as he walked, he'll say the canal was flat, like steel it was, that morning. It looked solid, like it had formed a border between his old self and his self now. Across on the other side, it looked to him as if, carved in tree trunks over there, there were faces, or bodies, fixed and distant and naked. The more he looked, the more he was reminded of things he should have tried to forget. And the air was strange, and beneath his feet, there'd been other things: a used condom, a couple of spent needles, and in places he'll say he felt the canal looking back at him, through him.

He smoked his cigarette down as far as he could, down to the filter, and it felt like breathing in shards of metal – needles, perhaps – and he loved it, that feeling. When his chest rattled, he coughed with a sound like a smack. And the water blushed as he spat into it.

The canal is carved in black against the landscape. When you're there, when you're next to it – just being near it – you can often feel it bolstered up, you can often feel a build-up of strength you didn't know it had, but look closely. It doesn't last. And you'll see a gradual loss of something. Sensation, perhaps. It's like it gets distressed sometimes. Like it has some kind of personality change. Like it's incapable of anything like happiness. There's a chemical flush you just can't explain. It's profound. There's a bus station nearby, and it casts out a forensic type of light for most of the day. The effect of the late-flowering bedding plants along the sweep of the footpath there, yellow and limp against the whitish grey concrete, is even more brutal than the light. The colours, the look, seem to make the smell of burnt fat from the town almost inevitable, though all of Stourbridge's smells seem to exist against another type of background aroma: the canal, most likely. It's a subtle kind of decay, like washing, wet, and having been left in the washing machine too long. Isabelle smelt it. And she hesitated, as if to look, as if she'd needed to stop for a moment to take the scene in, but it was only for a moment. By the time she'd descended into the subway, the air had begun to thin out. Nearer to town, the air is thinner, seems thinner, had seemed thinner then. A low wind had pushed empty packets, pages of newsprint, cartons, against walls. When she'd emerged into the High Street, there was a sense of vulgarity about the shape of her, about the redness of her coat. The cold had made her eyes water, but she wouldn't realise until later about the state of her eyeliner.

Gamble will say that he'd wanted to tell Carolyn about Hannah immediately. He'd wanted to be honest. Something like that. He'd wanted to be, but he wasn't. The problem was that Hannah had made him different. She'd made him behave differently towards Carolyn, and towards Isabelle. She'd changed him. After that time in the car, when he'd come home and had ended up in the kitchen by himself, he'd tried to rationalise it. At first, he'd thought she'd made him realise what was missing, that she'd highlighted what he hadn't got. And then it was, he thought, perhaps just the novelty value of her. He'll say she wasn't pretty at all. In fact, there was an ugliness about her. He'll say she had an almost permanent slight frown that made her face asymmetrical. Good side, bad side, he thought. Though, actually, he thought, perhaps both sides were bad. It made him wonder about himself, about whether he felt love, whether it was love he was feeling, or desire, or lust, or what. He still feels that now. In the end, he let six, seven months pass. He'd heard nothing more from Hannah. He'd found a new intimacy with himself, carrying the secret of her around with him, her presence still tangible, so a new routine melted into him. In that time, he'll say he gradually stopped worrying about what the post might contain – letters to him, or worse, to Carolyn from Hannah, is what he'd worried about at first – and he'd stopped jumping up out of his seat when someone knocked at the door, or a car slowed down outside the house. It was the time when he'd briefly given up smoking and drinking, he'd lost weight, he'd googled Buddhism. Occasionally, he caught sight of his reflection in his computer screen, or the window of his classroom, and thought he looked okay. So, it had been six, seven months, maybe even more. Carolyn had come downstairs on that day, looking, he thought, old, older, even then. It had seemed, he'll say, as though she was ageing before his very eyes. She was carrying a newspaper. He'd been marking books at the kitchen table. He did it there as a show of how busy he was. Look how busy I am, he was saying, without saying. Look how hard I'm working. He implied it. He still felt like he had to prey on Carolyn's ideas of what he ought to be. He'd felt her looking at him, could smell that she was freshly showered. He'll say there was an awkward pause – there were always those – like she might be about to announce she'd just found a used tissue in the fridge or something. But she'd said, 'We'll need to decorate, soon.'

She'd taken to sniffing, on the verge of a cold all the time. She said, 'These bare walls make me feel scratchy. Wallpaper'd be better. We need to cover up the cracks, anyway.'

He'd nodded but carried on marking, as if it was a forensic process. He wanted to give the impression of it being all such a complex thing: marking, his work, all that. He wanted it to seem like it was all so important, and by extension, that he was.

She said, 'And can you smell that? It's damp. Coming from somewhere.'

He couldn't smell it and he tried not to look up, but he could sense her prowling about as if she had no words that could describe how bad it was. He could hear the sound of fingernails against skin.

'And anyway,' she said, and she'd sat down opposite him, at the table. 'It'd add some . . .'

He'll say how he looked across at her, that it was unusual, this sitting down and talking, even then. She was looking around the room, around the ceiling, not at him. In her hand she held a rolled-up newspaper and she was rotating her wrist as if she was conducting a piece of music, and he could see red marks on her forearm where she'd scratched.

'Add some?' he said.

He'll say she did that thing with her mouth, like an upside down smile, or a gurn. She shrugged, said, 'Value.'

'It'd add value?' he said. 'What? Decorating?'

They were just people, talking, he thought.

'Well, you never know,' she said. 'We might want to sell up or something.'

She sniffed. He put his pen down on the table.

'Sell up?' he said. 'Sell this place?'

She seemed to take a long breath in and looked at him blankly. 'Greg,' she said. 'You want to live in the Black Country all your life?'

He noticed she had a stain on her T-shirt. She'd spilt something down there. Food, he thought. An uncertain line of mayonnaise or a drip of ketchup right about where her cleavage would be. He shuddered without realising it, and wasn't sure what to make of her tone.

'Do you want to move then?' he said. He didn't know what to say.

She gave him the slightest look, then blotted it out. She said, 'Look.' And she placed the newspaper on top of the book he'd been marking, splayed her hand out on it to straighten it out. He hadn't seen her hand so close to him for a long time. He'll say he hadn't realised she wore nail polish.

'The property pages, in the middle. Have a look.'

She got up from the table then and it, or the chair, moved sharply across the floor. Gamble will say he thought, good

God, she moves like an earthquake, and he had to stop the exercise books from falling off the table. She said something else as she left, something about him doing it when he had time. It had been words within a hissing sibilance of an inward breath. Whatever it was that she said, it came at him like a dry powder. He thought, briefly, about Buddhism and about kindness and about patience, but there was gravel in his throat. He neatened up the pile of books on the table, picked up the newspaper, licked his finger, turned the pages. He'd look through it, he decided, just to say he had. He was surprised Carolyn was interested in moving, but this was a local newspaper, so, he was thinking, she doesn't want to move far. She'd never mentioned it before. It made him wonder what else she didn't mention. And he was thinking just that, when he saw the photograph, the article. He'd tasted the newsprint on his finger and had placed it, the tip of his finger, on the next page, on the photograph there. It was a photograph of Hannah. Her hair looked a little longer, less of a mess, but the look of her was the same, the not-quite smile and the asymmetrical face. How much was she going to change in that time anyway? Gamble will tell how he felt that gravel rise in his throat, just seeing her face, that face, staring out at him. It looked like some kind of selfie she might have taken and placed on some social networking site, slightly high angle, slightly pouty, the fingers loosely touching the chin. He could see, just about, the fingers curled round, the fingernails, bitten. And the headline: 'Body of Local Woman found in Canal.' He'd smeared spit across her neck, across that collar bone of hers, and the paper wrinkled a little there. He could hear his breathing, like some kind of animal might breathe. It was as if he'd lifted slightly out of the seat. 'Fuck,' he said. 'Fucking hell.' And he realised he was, in fact, standing. 'Fucking hell.' He remembers he was shouting, he was shaking the newspaper with both hands, like he was trying to throttle it, or wake it up. Then, he'll tell how a voice came at him from the doorway. The outline of a child. Isabelle. 'Daddy,' she said. And he wondered who she was talking to, and she was giving him the slightest look, then blotting it out. He remembers, he sat down, heavy. A couple of the exercise books slid off onto the floor. And the pen. His lips were quite suddenly dry, and when he spoke, the parting of them sounded like paper tearing. He'll tell how he remembers exactly what he said. He said, 'What a bitch.' And he looked straight at Isabelle.

Of course, that was years ago. Recently, he managed to get his old desk-top computer working, managed to get it to connect to the internet and there'd been a dull glow that he'd found comforting, safe, spreading across the desk, the ashtray, the carpet, the bed there. The Old Doll Factory, Gamble thought, when he looked at it from the spare room, made outside seem like it was another planet, or maybe just otherworldly, or as if it just belonged to him, no-one else. It was the way it cut an irregular shape out of the picture. He couldn't, for the life of him, think why he hadn't really noticed it before. And that fascinated him. He hadn't taken any pills that day – he'd started back-of-the-counter painkillers, ones you have to ask the pharmacist for – just to see what would happen, and he'd found he felt more polished, like there was no vanishing point to him. Like there might be an endless flow of him. He'd felt like he ought to be more anxious than he was, but couldn't muster it, the anxiety, despite being constantly aware of his heartbeat. He'll say he found the word 'rubatosis' on the internet and will say now that summed up how he was feeling. There was a sense within him of possibility that he didn't want anything to suppress, a bit like being on the verge of falling in love. He wished he wanted a drink. Brandy. Just because of the coolness of the look of someone drinking brandy. But he didn't have any in the house, he didn't think, and anyway, basically he felt fine. He'll say how he was wearing his old shirt, the denim one with the missing button, and that felt good, to him. There was music, he'll say, quiet, dulled but familiar, and, at the time, he'll say it might have been coming from Isabelle's room: an irregular, gentle thud overlaid with monotone drawl, the sort she seemed to like lately. Wherever it was coming from, even that offered comfort to him, just then.

He'd spent the day walking, down and away and along the Black Country wilderness bordered by the canal. He could still smell the air of it on him, on his shirt, his skin. It reminded him of when he was a boy, that smell, and it made him feel all that promise that had been stolen away was, in fact, still there, buried deep, but still there. His feet ached, his toes, and he thought about buying walking shoes, or proper running shoes, and taking up running again, getting fit. He rubbed his chin. He hadn't shaved, and this, all of this, made him feel outside of himself. The day, though, was going. Now, in the distance, the hills were getting fuzzy, and, closer, there were no lights in any of the windows opposite. Saturday evening, he thought, and he thought the girl would probably be out, and that made him feel a plunge of disappointment, or age. Beneath him, he felt the front door of his house click closed, and the top of Carolyn's head zig-zagged into view. Instinctively, he stepped back from the window, but not far enough so that he couldn't see her. The top of her head, her scalp, was visible in a fine white line. It seemed to him that she'd put some sort of vaguely purple colour on her hair and from that distance, it gave her a slightly vampish look. He watched her get into her car, struggle to get reverse gear, and drive off, eventually. She hadn't looked up, and he'd been able to see the plump of her knees alternate in a spasm of irritation. He supposed she was going to her mother's. The exhaust of her car coughed a line of grey against the silver of the road, or vice versa, he couldn't quite tell. As soon as she was out of sight, he levered open the window and let the air bite at him. He lit a cigarette and he'll say smoking like this reminded him of being a teenager, of the process of striking a match, cupping his hand around the flame, of inhaling the smoke, then positioning himself so that he could blow all of it out into the street, of blowing it all away, of being only half sure never to have been found out. It had been all about the secret, the danger, the crime of it, smoking, then. When he smoked now, he felt the crackle of enjoyment still, but Carolyn's disapproval tainted it. All that stuff about setting an example to Isabelle, etcetera, sometimes spoilt it. So he blew smoke out into the early evening, like he was young again, like it was a secret.

The day was going. The Old Doll Factory he looked at through this smoke of his. Every now and then, it looked like it was a picture he'd smeared with spit, or maybe just licked. Streetlights flickered on, pretty much in unison, three of them, so everything looked like a film set, or a touched-up photograph, and he was an actor in it all. He was the protagonist. He'll tell how briefly, he thought back to his university days. He'd smoked pot in those days, he and his friends. *Pot.* He thought about the word and wondered whether people even called it that now. He'd heard pupils at his school mumbling

about 'weed', and had thought about that change of termi-
nology. Weed, to him, meant second- or even third-rate
rubbish no-one wanted or should want, and he had no idea
what 'Skunk' was. Pot, though, *Pot* meant a safe container
– a vessel – of friendship, of creativity. He thought about
that, about those times he and his friends – what exactly had
happened to them? – used to get hold of something really
good to smoke and had spent nights smoking it surrounded
by tea-candles, listening to David Gilmore and talking about
important things, talking about poetry, writing poetry. Even
Carolyn had tried it once, smoking pot with them, reluctantly, as he remembered, but it had made her sick, and he'd
thought that apt, even at the time. Still. He thought back
to those days, spending hours in the library researching the
Romantic poets. God, he thought, where's he gone, that young
guy reading William Blake and having ideas and smoking pot?
Fleetingly, he wondered if he went into Birmingham, Digbeth,
say, or even somewhere closer, Lye or Cradley, whether he'd
be able to get hold of something good to smoke. He had no
contacts, of course, and had no idea of how you'd go about
it these days, and he doubted he could bring himself to even
ask for, let alone smoke, *weed*. His thoughts, the colour of
them, were starting to turn, from streetlight orange, through
vampish purple, to blue. Grim, he was thinking, how time
changes things. Sad, in the old-fashioned sense. And it was
this he was thinking when the car pulled up to a stop outside
his house. He squinted at it through his smoke-breath, heard
them cut the engine in an undramatic way, saw them get out:
a woman, from the driver's seat, and a man from the passenger
side. They seemed to be working simultaneously. One of them
opened the back door of the car. A young woman, with the

darkest eyes and wearing a red coat, got out of the back seat. He thought he heard someone say Isabelle's name and something about a key, or home, or being safe. The man seemed to be placing a cap on his head. Everything was hi-vis, like there'd be an expectation of violence or resistance. In Gamble's head things were only just beginning to slot together, like a difficult jigsaw. He'll say now, you only expect to see what you expect to see. The word on the side of the car, the thing on the top of the roof, sneaking blue at him. They were walking up the drive, the three of them. He could see the top of their heads, the way they'd placed their caps on, and Isabelle, a line of white scalp, he could see it – it was her – with her red coat, and he could hear the key in the door, and someone calling his name, calling him 'Mister Gamble'. And he was thinking how he hadn't even recognised Isabelle, at first, how he'd thought she was just some young woman. He felt a little jabbing pain where he thought his heart might be, and moved automatically, stabbing the cigarette out in the ashtray next to the computer. Carolyn's knees, irritably alternating, trying to get reverse gear, flashed across his thoughts, and a little pot of guilt upturned in his mind. They were calling him, still, calling up at him: 'Mister' and 'Sir' as he half-ran out across the landing. And the car, the police car, he could hear it from there, was ticking as it cooled across his drive.

Gamble didn't believe it, about Hannah, back then, not at first. He'll say he remembers quickly closing the newspaper, and standing up. He'll say he remembers trembling a little. He'd said what he'd said and young Isabelle had looked stunned more than shocked, but he wasn't paying any attention to her, he'll say that now, in fact, he thought she was in the way. He'll say he felt his stomach squeeze and everything inside him tense up. He remembers getting past Isabelle, making his way to the upstairs bathroom, locking the door, finding himself pissing wildly against the porcelain. It wasn't so much that it seemed right, as it was the only thing he could do, he couldn't stop it. And his hands were shaking – which was another thing he couldn't stop – and piss was all of a sudden all down the outside of the toilet and he'll say the smell was odd, it was the smell of something acidic. No. Not acidic. Something sharp, like pear-drops, maybe. Pear-drops and metal and bone and blood. And sap. The smell that sap makes when it's bleeding from a branch. That sticky, piny smell. But he was telling himself he was being ridiculous, hysterical. He was telling himself to stop it, but he just couldn't. He remembers placing one hand against the wall there, to steady himself, and letting the other hand lock around his balls and feeling the moist skin there contract and float at the same time, like the feel of damp paper over beads of glass. He'll say he should have known then, but he was pissing all over the floor, all over his shoes. Looking back, he would say that, at the time, he had thought that what Hannah had done was more cunning than clever. It was his punishment, he decided. She was punishing him, he thought. That she'd told him, she wouldn't say anything, had been significant. He'd thought she'd planned what she would do all along. It had been his sword of Damocles, hanging over his head. He'd thought she'd left it all that time – six months, seven – and she'd plotted, he thought. He didn't think she could possibly be dead, she was only twenty-two. He'll say he thought twenty-two-year-olds don't commit suicide. He'll say he thought it must have been a lie, a ploy. He remembers standing in his bathroom, half-naked, amber pools like modern art here and there on the laminate flooring. He'll say he snapped off some toilet paper and wiped it across the floor, that it was soaked into dark orange, almost red, immediately, that it was cold on the palm of his hand, that it made a childish 'blat' when he threw it into the toilet. He'll say he knew Carolyn would be beside herself if he'd left a mess there, but can't remember if he cleaned it all up, or if he washed his hands, or took his shoes off. He was being ridiculous, hysterical, for sure.

Looking back now, he'll say that for weeks, months perhaps, the sense of disbelief made him sure he saw her – Hannah, he's talking about – prowling around outside his house, or the corridors at work, or waiting next to his car in the car park there. Once he thought he'd seen her going into the Head Teacher's office, and a couple of times when he'd been home by himself, someone had rung the doorbell, and he'd hidden behind the kitchen door, out of sight.

He'd torn the article out of the newspaper, and he'll say he carried it around with him, in his trouser pocket. He read and re-read it. For a few days, he read it like it was a sacrament, even though reading it made him feel sick, made him sweat. He felt it, the sweat, running down his back. She was torturing him, he thought. He thought, at the time, she really is dangerous, he just didn't think she could be dead. He'll say something about the way the ink on the paper, the dots or whatever they are, seemed to give out a different kind of danger from the eyes. Looking at it, the picture there, seemed to Gamble like a passage into another type of world. He concentrated on the asymmetry of her face, the heavy weight on the slope of her shoulders he hadn't noticed before. He examined her face as if through a microscope, he couldn't help it, he just didn't believe she was dead, and then, at work, in the toilets there, he'll tell how he tore it up, the article, and flushed it away. Later, at home, he sat at his then new desk-top computer, and browsed around until he found her profile on Facebook. He felt defeated. Keep in mind, this was four years ago. What was going on in his mind? Fear, of course, yes, but what else? Anger, for sure. He'll say now that he scrolled through photograph after photograph of her profile. He was clicking through them all until his wrist, his hand, started to hurt. It's like she has nothing to hide, he was thinking, like she has nothing to lose. And every picture, every photograph, revolted him more. He could see in each one, it was like she'd tried to keep everything about herself the same, like an exact formula: the same tilt of the head, the same smile, the same slope of the shoulders. But behind that, what he saw was a constructed vulnerability loaded, for sure, with dynamite. And through each image, like a magic-eye picture, he could see himself, a reflection of himself that is – a reflection of his face, simply, in the glass of the screen – like a hungry, brutish thing. And it had felt to him then, that *he* was still the one balancing on a tightrope of need. He'll say he was reduced to looking at the screen through slatted fingers, afraid of being found out, and then deleting his internet history in case anyone else – Carolyn – should check. He'll say he felt, just then, that, dead or alive, Hannah had outsmarted him.

Carolyn, even Carolyn, noticed the change in him. He could tell because although she didn't mention moving house again, she'd taken to snagging her glance at him for longer, leaning against the kitchen work surface, arms folded, watching him move away from her. It made him tip-toe about the place, like he was trying to disappear himself. It made him pick at the skin around his thumbs so they bled. He'll tell how it made him worry.

Gamble will think back to a specific moment. He ruminates on it now. He'll say he was in the spare room and didn't hear the footfalls, specifically, but he was aware of them, and by the time the door was opened and the breathing was beside him, it must have seemed like he was staring at a blank screen. Children have a way of making an entrance into a room that no adult can.

'I knew you were in here, I could see the light.' Isabelle was excited, breathing fast, and brought with her that pre-adolescent smell, it was always all over her in those days.

'You shouldn't just burst in. I'm busy,' he'd said. 'I'm working.'

He remembers he could still feel sweat shimmering down his back and knew his voice hadn't come out like he'd wanted it to. He lifted his arm to soothe the irritation of cooling at the back of his neck, and Isabelle winced, he remembers, as if she'd thought he might smack her, but he relaxed, or tried to and scratched the back of his head.

He'll say now that he felt frightened of his own child, at least, that's what he'll say he remembers.

Isabelle had stolen, or had tried to steal, make-up. Lipstick, black. And condoms.

'Shoplifting?' Gamble said to her, in front of the police officers. 'You're shoplifting now, then?'

They were in the kitchen, standing. All four of them. Isabelle and the two police officers had formed a sort of mass of something. Defence, perhaps. Or protection. It made Gamble feel like he should have been less fearful and more menacing, more aggressive. He felt like he ought to have upended the table or smashed a mug, like they might have expected it of him. He didn't know for sure. Isabelle's body, he noticed, seemed to be pitching backwards away from him and he found he was, in fact, standing, wringing his hands as if he was washing them. He was trying to remember her as that pre-adolescent kid, but the person standing in front of him was a woman now.

'Unacceptable,' he heard himself say. 'Shameful, Isabelle.'

One of the police officers cleared her throat, and Gamble took that to mean she wanted more of that, more chastising.

'I'm ashamed of you,' he said. 'And I hope you're ashamed of yourself.'

Both police officers were looking down at their feet as if he was speaking to them, or as if he had to try harder to reprimand Isabelle more. So Gamble said, 'Stealing is a disgusting thing to do. Absolutely disgusting.'

Isabelle, he remembers, seemed to straighten very slowly, like she'd just realised she might be carrying a massive burden across her shoulders. Gamble said, 'We're not that kind of family here.' And he thought one of the police officers nodded. Isabelle's face was puffed up, red. He could, and would, have gone on like that, but one of the police officers raised a hand as if stopping traffic, as if that was enough.

When the police left, he saw them to the door like they'd been invited guests. It was a show for any neighbours who might have been looking. As he watched the police car drive away, thankful for the dark, he'd tell you he was thinking how easy it would be to just walk away, just then, how much he felt this life was not what he deserved, not what he had planned. He wasn't angry, not really. What he felt was buried beneath a pile of responsibility he didn't want. He walked out, down, off his drive, onto the pavement, and then into the road. Standing, watching the police car take the corner at the top there, he started listing all the things, in his head, that he did not deserve. The urge to walk, or run, perhaps, was there, and he'll say now, that he would have done, he would have walked away just then, or run, if she hadn't appeared. The girl from the building opposite. She'd appeared, or seemed to, from nowhere, and was standing across the street from him. She must have been returning from shopping, that's what she looked like. She was carrying two large bags. And she must have seen him and wondered what was going on. And she'd stood looking at him, uncertain at first, then, when he didn't move, she'd said – and it was quietly said – 'Are you alright?' and he'd said 'No, actually, I'm not.'

She'd wanted a puppy, or a kitten, Isabelle had. Carolyn had said that she could have one.

In other circumstances, in circumstances where he hadn't been laden down with guilt and worry, he would have disapproved, would have refused point-blank, would have said something about the mess, or the smell, or yet more responsibility. There would have been an argument. But he had – he has – a way of sounding sincere when he needs to, and anyway, just then, he could see the worth of being generous, of conceding. He knew, though, that he had to walk quite carefully, that Carolyn would be expecting a level of abrasion.

He'll tell how afterwards, downstairs, with the article still folded in his trouser pocket, he said, 'Well, if that's what she wants, I suppose.' And his tone faltered, wasn't quite right, it must have been that, because Carolyn turned, squinted at him.

'I'd absolutely love a puppy. I really would.' Isabelle was delighted.

'What's got into you?' Carolyn said, and he said, 'Nothing,' a bit too quickly.

'Yes, there is,' she said. He could see the scientist in her then, she was examining every bit of his face. 'You hate animals. And you're being weird.'

Gamble let out a sound like a laugh, but not quite, and found he couldn't look her in the eye.

'Christ,' he said, and he could feel sweat, again, on his neck, down his back. The value of an argument struck him. His mouth couldn't find words for a second or two. 'Well,' he said. 'Yes, I do. I mean I don't. Like animals. You know that. Dogs are horrible creatures. And cats . . .' He was just saying words, trying to find something to stoke a little confrontation. But Carolyn was staring straight at him.

'How come you're being like this?' she said.

And he was thinking, this is ridiculous, and he wiped his hand across his forehead, was shocked to feel the grease there, the heat. Carolyn's eyes fluttered across the action he did, then down to his shoes.

'What's up with you?' she said. She seemed to be squaring up to him. It, she, was starting to terrify him.

'Don't know,' he said, and the proximity of her squeezed the air between them, so he suddenly became aware of the smell of himself. 'I might, maybe, go to bed. Might be one of my heads coming on.'

He made his eyelids flicker, as if the light bulb was suddenly toxic.

'I'll go for a lie down, I think.'

In some ways, he hoped she could see the damp spreading

across the back of his shirt as he retreated. And as he started climbing the stairs, he said, in a little, weak voice, 'I'll just try and get this work done first, this marking.' She didn't answer.

In the spare room, he leaned on the door to close it. That air in there, it had an outside damp quality to it, though it might just have been something coming from him. It, and the rest of it, of course, made him shiver. He tried to avoid seeing himself behind the grub of the mirror of the dressing table there because it would have been hard to argue with the logic of his reflection. He opened the curtains a bit more, and even that little movement sent dust into the air, and thick motes lingered. Outside, when he looked, the sky was already the colour of ash, it was impossible to tell whether it was early or late. The inner workings of him twisted a little when he flicked the computer screen on again. It was, he thought then, quite like the onset of a migraine, looking at that screen. Social networking he had no experience of back then. To him, it had seemed like an available sneak, like it could be a treasure trove, or a junk shop. He found Hannah's profile again. Even the look of her name put him across into dishonesty. Look at those words, he thought. He seemed to feel them like a magnetic force. And blood, he felt blood in his cheeks, his ears, his fingertips. The smell of himself was overwhelming. He was looking at photographs of her, half-looking, now, more confident. I'm a peeping Tom now, he was thinking, but he didn't stop. Light from his screen was reflecting back into his glasses, catching the edge of things like some kind of corona. If he'd have taken a photograph of himself just then, he knew he'd have looked his age, and he'd have looked professorial, tired, tightly wound, alone. There was, he thought, a grit about the jawline. It's ingrained. It's more than an expression he has.

He felt his fingertips on the keyboard, and then off again. He wanted, he needed, to send a message, or thought he did. How many versions did he think of? All of them wrong. Either wheedling and twee or too brusque, and he realised he was trying too hard to find the right way to put it, and would, if he wasn't careful, poke at demons. In the end he'll say all he could think of was: 'Leave me alone.'

Talking about that now, he knows he was sending a message to a dead girl. And even now, he doesn't know exactly why.

Despite the weather, the canal seemed flat. It was possible to think you could walk on it, or write on it. It was as if it, the water, was the only calm thing amongst the panic of trees. Leaves trembled, and branches, like they might be about to lose control. The wind down there flustered everything, except the water. Rain had frightened the earth – it had just started to rain – and now the towpath had started to become a slick of mud and bleeding. And the water in the canal, still as it was, thick as it was, was the colour of the blood of strangers. You can take shelter under a tree – an oak or something similar – because rain can happen. It could – it can – leave you shivering. There were people hanging around down there. Young types. Too young. Looking at their watches, seeming to think, or wish, they could slow time, or stop it. If you'd looked at them, you'd have seen it: worry, or something, draining colour from their face and their eyes looked large, larger, like something inside their heads, hot and urgent, was pressing. One of them trembled, distracted by a phone. Steps, uncertain but quick, light had slipped about in the sludge and had caught in the tangle of roots, and though there'd been no loss of control, limbs had twisted, had become loose-looking, and even the overhanging ivy and gorse had been weak under the grip. There'd been a fall, a closing of eyes as if seeing the sludge and blistering earth like that would have been even more painful.

Imagine, a body recoiling as it falls, ready for the feeling of the way the earth, or water, would tear at the skin.

'No, actually, I'm not.' Gamble remembers saying it again, to the girl. 'I'm not alright, no.' The sky was thick black, moonless. Lights from the houses at the top of the road cut out spiteful holes from it, the blackness. The police car had disappeared, but he thought it might suddenly reappear, that it might have turned round over the brow of the hill. He wanted to be ready for it.

She, the girl, tilted her head very slightly. She was standing on the pavement, looking at him. He'll tell how pale she looked. She said, 'Well, you're standing in the middle of the road, so . . .' The carrier bags she was holding made a stretching sound. She seemed to wait a second before she took one pace forward. But it was as if he was beginning to sink, or be torn, out of himself. That's how he remembers it. As if he had capsized, was drowning. He managed to say, 'I'm not alright.' This was not the way he'd envisaged talking to this girl for the first time. He was battling an unbearable feeling of needing to exhale, like he was underwater, having held his breath for too long. The more she stood there watching him, the worse it became. He felt his legs buckling and he imagined sugar melting in hot water. Falling onto the tarmac, knees first, felt sacrificial. It was too late for dignity. The girl placed the carrier bags on the roadside. He saw her approach him like an onrush of pain, and he felt her hands on him, oddly warm. To him, then, it was too real, too soon. He'll tell how he felt his eyelids fluttering and how he struggled to focus on the girl as she seemed to lift him, like he was a marionette, despite the size of her. His glasses slipped down his nose – it must have been the sweat – and he didn't seem to be able to work out how to push them back into place. This was a new fragility he was feeling, and he was stumbling, trying to compose himself, trying to say a mix of gratitude and apology, and ending up mumbling something simpering and blurry and stupid. He didn't resist her though. He'll tell you that for certain. Even in the state he was, he went with the flow of it. He went with her – she took him – into the Old Doll Factory. He'll say he remembers being put, manhandled, really, into the lift – there was a lift he didn't noticed before – of leaning against her, of no-one speaking, but of feeling this denseness, and an over-warmth he could only just see, or feel, in his peripheral vision. His shoes, the toes of them, were different. They were scuffed, is all, he realises now, but he couldn't think of that word, 'scuffed'. The word was on the tip of his tongue and he couldn't quite get it. Things were rushing towards him at speed, or away from him, he couldn't work it out – it might have just been the feeling of the lift moving. That he couldn't control it, or control anything, made him yearn to be back home, in his kitchen, or better, in the spare room, or back in time. She, the girl, was saying, 'What's your name?' And he was shaking, surprised at her voice, that she had this thin, local accent, but there was something else. 'What's your name?' Her face was close to his. He could have kissed her if he'd wanted, but he couldn't focus on her. 'Greg,' he said. To him he sounded drunk. 'Stay with me, Greg,' she said. 'Stay with me.' And just hearing that, the way she said it, made him feel like crying. He was starting to feel, even then, he'll say, like he was being eaten alive. By the time they were outside the door of this girl's flat, he was sobbing, he remembers that. He could feel her hand cupping his elbow and she was saying something about a drink, and then somehow they were in and the door was closed and there was a glass in his hand. Brandy, he thought. It smelt like brandy. Or whisky. He didn't know. He wasn't that kind of drinker. The glass was dirty around the rim. Lipstick. He could see it. Kissed smudges around the rim of the glass. She, the girl, was standing in the far corner, or seemed to be. She'd lit a cigarette and was smoking it in long, slow breaths. A couple of times, as she stood there, she spat out little bits of tobacco from the very tip of her tongue. 'Thip,' she seemed to be saying. Things like that he remembers sharply. And he'll say he'd never seen anything so cheap looking, or cool, in his entire life.

She said something, but he couldn't hear or see her mouth because of the smoke, he thought. He just couldn't see her clearly. And he said, 'Sorry, what?'

'Drink it,' she said. It was like she was observing him from afar, as if he might be an unexploded bomb, or an alien.

He took a sip, brandy. And he heard her say, 'All of it.' And so he swallowed it all and managed to thank her with breath hot and deep. He felt the grease of the lipstick on his lips and wiped his mouth with his fingertips. His breath was burning. He'll tell how he felt a continual need to thank her, and apologise, and she seemed to let him, as if, in doing so, she was monitoring him. He couldn't make out the features of her face. 'My glasses,' he said, and it felt as if he'd suddenly woken up and he was feeling across his nose, his eyelids. He'll tell you he thought it was partly the brandy making him feel like that.

'Here,' she said, and she sat down next to him, placed his

glasses on him, on his face, and there was a fumble, a touching of her fingers and his fingers on the back of her hand as he put the glasses on properly. The smell of old smoke and perfume was so close to his face, he could have eaten it.

They were sitting on a sofa, he realised. He'll tell you all his thoughts were quickly coming into focus then, like a photograph developing at double speed, and he couldn't even look at her face, being already beyond gratitude, and embarrassment. But he'd been left feeling sharp, sharpened, on guard, perhaps. He knew himself, and he knew only too well that his recovery would be so swift that he needed to pretend he was still unwell, at least for a little while. These episodes of his, they were starting to happen more often then, or at least, this is what he'll say. He put his hand on his chest, sat forward, giving the impression he might be sick, actually vomit, at any moment. His glasses were smudged with fingerprints, and there was a scratch across one of the lenses. He had to struggle to look around him. The flat was smaller than he'd imagined, the room he was in was small, that is. There were candles of different colours, burnt down and melted on top of wine bottles and it reminded him of his student digs, or a cheap restaurant. There were odd ornaments, things he couldn't make out on the mantelpiece, scattered packs of cigarettes on shelves, a coffee table in front of him with circular stains where mugs had spilt and an ashtray with a couple of stubbed-out cigarettes. There were muddy foot prints, some were his, he guessed, on bare floor boards. There were silk flowers in a vase, and garish patterned wallpaper on one wall. Underwear had been draped over a radiator. Above that, the Venetian blinds were slightly skewed as if they'd been closed too quickly. A baseball cap had been left on the window sill there, and he could see the emblem, the embroidered patch was of an orchid, white, he realised. Music filtered in from a distance, but Gamble couldn't tell what it was exactly, it might have been the sort Isabelle liked lately. And everything was tainted with smoke. To him, there was an air of carnival and sex in there that was almost ceremonial. The girl seemed to sense the change in him, and, as if she was no longer needed, placed her pack of cigarettes on the table, stood up. He'll say he felt an instant, and ridiculous, sense of abandonment. He thought perhaps she realised the threat of taking a stranger into her home like she had, and wanted to put things right. This was not how he had imagined things would happen between them. He still had the glass in his hand. He thumbed the lipstick off the rim. When he looked up, the girl seemed to be moving things or rearranging ornaments on shelves, touching them, more like: little pottery creatures, a jar of something, a tiny jug, a photograph frame. She was adjusting them, making them point in a different direction, it seemed to him. She said something, or sighed, and it surprised him when she bent down and flicked some sort of gas fire on full. It was like they'd gone back in time. When she spoke, she said, 'You're shivering.' And he said, 'Yes.' And he might have apologised again if she hadn't sat on the floor in front of him, picked up the pack of cigarettes.

'Do you mind if I have one of those?' he said, and he watched her arms, her hands, the skin, whiter than he'd ever seen before. She had a clumsy way of doing things, he noticed. Uncareful summed up everything about her. And when he looked at her face, she was as young as he'd imagined her to be, for sure. There was a paleness to her skin. He studied her; he couldn't stop himself. He looked at her eyes, her skin, and couldn't help thinking of petals, overlapping, resupinate. The teeth, or part of the front two, he could see as a little triangle, and the tongue shimmered, like she was saying something he couldn't hear. When he looked closely at the rest of her – and she seemed to be letting him – her hair was, in fact, almost blonde, dirty blonde, he'll say now, and she did keep pushing strands of it behind her ear. Every movement she made was jerky, so it felt to Gamble that if he blinked, he'd miss something important. It looked like she was constantly irritated about something or other. She looks cartoonish, he thought, but he'll say now that it made him want to draw her, or paint her, or write a poem about her, or a novel. He bitterly regretted wearing his wedding ring, and placed his right hand over it as if giving thanks. When she lit his ciga-rette, it was with a match, and the smell of it made Gamble think of nightclubs and freedom and girls he'd known when he was a student. It could, everything about this situation he was in, he knew, take him to an intensely uncareful place indeed.

'I haven't drunk brandy in . . .' He laughed, put the glass down on the table.

She sat with her legs curled beneath her. She must have kicked off her shoes, he thought. He could see her feet. He couldn't tell what she was thinking, but the way she looked at him, it was as if she was experiencing the planning of a response.

'There's wine,' she said, but didn't move. 'In the kitchen. Only cheap stuff, but still.' And her lips glistened.

She leaned back, as if what she'd said was a challenge to him. It was a child-like movement, and he thought she was either unaware of how it made her seem, or shrewdly unconcerned about the effect it might have. He tried to keep his eyes on her face, her eyes, not her lips or her body.

'Okay,' he said. 'Right. Wine.'

She stood up, as if someone had unwound her; her face was saying nothing as she walked out of the room. He wondered for a second if she was in some kind of trance. The tables seemed to have turned. She was making him feel reckless. *She* was making him feel this. Wine, he thought, seemed an infinitely good idea.

'Look, I don't know if you know, but.' He tried not to look at her, to be cool. He moved towards where she was, he leaned against the door frame of her kitchen. He could see silvery stains on the wall just there, like something had been thrown, or splashed. He'll say, she seemed to be quickly wiping something away from the worktop with a sponge, brown from use. When she saw him, she stopped, waited for a second, then picked up a wine glass, held it with both hands. She leaned back, physically, as if removing her *self* from the potential of what might be said, but her face, her expression remained interested, and he liked that. He liked the childishness of it. He liked that she could be brash one minute, then not; close to and far away at almost the same time. He cleared his throat, said, 'I saw you. I saw something happen to you.' It was like he couldn't bring himself to say exactly what, and he hesitated. He was, he knew, forming a conspiracy with her. And, really, he didn't want her to fill in the gap. He'll say he wanted there to be this unspoken knowledge between them, as if he was – what was he? – some kind of guardian angel to her, or could be. So he walked to the far end of the room then, picking up and putting down some of her ornaments, looking at the candles, only half looking at the jar, which looked to him to contain tiny little odd-shaped pearls, then standing, wanting and not wanting to look out of the window, his back to where she was. He slowed his movements, not graceful exactly, but as if he was thinking them through way ahead of time. He'll say, in truth, he was experiencing the whole situation more sharply than he could bear. He'll say he could feel her, even then, even at that moment *implanting* herself into him. He knew that. And he was letting her. And perhaps that's why he did what he did next. It's unclear exactly why, but he'll say he slipped his fingers between the slats of the venetian blinds. Maybe he intended just to check what it was like to see out, to just experience the seeing from there. But the road outside was smudged with the beginnings of a mist. He'd wished it had been a dense fog, so that he wouldn't have been able to see his house, his car. But he could. He could see the door of his house, still open, he could see coats hung up near the door, the light, the floor. Isabelle, he'll say, was a flash of dark in the corner there, and he felt a sudden mix of anger and sadness. And then car lights swept across the tarmac, slowed to a stop. Carolyn. He could have stayed where he was. He wanted to. He'll tell you that. He wanted to stay and drink cheap wine with this girl. He wanted to light one of those candles, smoke all those cigarettes. He'd felt they weren't quite on the edge of talking. But just the look of Carolyn's way, the way she slammed the car door, the way she half-ran up the drive, the way she glanced about and mouthed something to the half-light inside before closing the door, made him know he had to go.

And leaving that flat was like moving towards a harder reality. More than just *like*, it was a surety. He'd left like he was being chased. He'd called to the girl. Something about thanking her, something about having to go. He didn't hear her reply.

Follow the canal, the water. Walk out from Stourbridge and you'll eventually get to places where it looks like it's boiling, the water. Bubbles appear at the surface as if something there, deep down, something is surging up from the earth, rumbling up through the bones of it. That's the place where the earth seems oldest, frailest. That's the place where the skin of the earth is broken, picked at, damaged. The pain is loud. At times of the year when the day falls away quickly, anyone can be mistaken for anyone else, or anything else, down there, by the canal. There is a very particular type of blackness in the Black Country, so there aren't any shadows to speak of. Down there. It's not so much dark, exactly, as unlight. Some things try to cast long shadows, and the look of them can be overwhelming, brutal. Like the glass cone. It looks like a killing cone. It does. They light it up orange at night, and that makes it worse. And at times of the year when the day falls away quickly, and rain has fallen, and all the creases and pores in the earth have been filled or overfilled, the water turns iron-red, blood-red, and it runs into the canal. And people wait under narrow bridges, crouched and made smaller against arched bricks, as if the water itself, or the place, has manipulated time, or time has struggled and evolved differently, has rotated round people. It's easy to lose track of it, down there: time. But still, people wait – some people wait – crouched and made smaller, ready to pounce, watching the slow fading changes of light, or colour.

Walk out from Stourbridge at a certain time of year, and the water, the fact of it, moves the boundaries of everything you'd thought was right or real. Like an abstract thought you think you've understood but can't explain. And the water: it will sometimes look like it's boiling. And the scum on the surface breaches. But before it does, the bubbles look precious, like little pearls. Little tiny odd-shaped pearls.

Ask Gamble about Hannah, how he dealt with that, and he'll say he felt her blood was on his hands, under his fingernails and on the edges of his sleeves, yes. He'll tell how he told Carolyn, how he confessed. He'd rehearsed what to say, about Hannah that is: something about him making a mistake, something about being a fool. He was scared, but of what? He wasn't absolutely sure. Of losing the house, his daughter? Of coming clean? Clichés were the only thing he could think of. He remembers getting in deliberately late from work. A bad day – another one – because he couldn't get Hannah off his mind. Carolyn, he'll say, was sitting on the easy chair, furthest from the TV, where she always sat, even then, because of her eyesight. Her face was granulated with colour from something, some programme, she was watching. She had a kind of un-earthly smile on her face, like she was watching something she liked. She was slimmer then, Gamble will tell you, or looked slimmer in that light, but she looked like a mannequin, she was sitting so still. He remembers her hair, cut in a style he didn't like, fashionable at the time, scraped across her head in the way that some men use to conceal baldness, he'd thought. She hadn't moved, even though she must have heard him come in. In his house, he remembers a smell he wasn't used to, a smear of scent that he didn't remember being there before. The place was as quiet as distant thunder, he'd thought, but he'll say he knew then he had no choice but to tell her – he had to get it out of him, he'll say.

'Carolyn,' he said. He simply said her name like that. He was trembling. He'd been running through it all the way home, practising it, like a recitation, in the car. He stood on the threshold of the living room – the lounge – and his arrival, he noticed, had set a flickering pulse against the net curtains. Isabelle, he knew, was in bed, long asleep. He kept his hands clasped, like he was praying, but mainly to disguise the unsteadiness in them. 'I need to tell you something.'

He'd hoped the combination of his look, his tone, his movements, might have at least hinted at what he might be about to say.

She looked at him. He'll say she had this pleasant look on her face, a transitional look from seeing something she was enjoying to seeing something she knew she would not. She didn't say anything, and he thought, later, that was ept. He felt himself becoming formal, becoming a teacher, watching his step, being appropriate, thinking of the words to use. Later, he would realise, when thinking about why he'd told her then, that it was all about him. It was all about lifting the weight off his shoulders, and about being one step ahead of her, Carolyn, that is. He didn't want her to find out, or work it out. He wanted it to be *his* words she'd heard, his explanation. He wanted it to be on, and in, his terms. And he told her, Carolyn, what he wanted her to know, and left out the bits he did not. He didn't want any nasty surprises.

The odd thing was – there were several odd things – that, first, he managed to keep control of himself. His explanation, he thought, didn't come out in fierce gusts of self-deprecation or regret. It came out as facts, he thought. That was the first odd thing. More than that, was Carolyn's reaction. She didn't even switch off the TV, or move much, except to clench her fists. When he'd finished telling her what he wanted to about Hannah, it seemed to him that she thought there might even be a little more to say. There was a hesitation, a pause, when they both looked at each other, light from the TV dotting across both their faces. And then Carolyn said, 'Are you leaving?' And he said, 'God, no. No.' What had crossed his mind was mainly to do with finances: the house, the mortgage, the car loans, the general tiresomeness of having to find somewhere else to live. He realised he was only thinking of practicalities. Carolyn, when he thought about it later, had the same quiet superiority as Hannah had, but the difference was that it seemed she, Carolyn, was fending off any prospect of drama. Her internal thermostat, he thought, lowered, and he couldn't help admiring that about her. Eventually, she'd said, 'Is that all? Is that it?' and he'd said, 'Yes.' 'There's nothing else?' she'd said. And he'd shaken his head, emptied out, except for a few details. Carolyn had stood up, and for a second he'd thought she was going to slap him, and he'd braced himself when she approached him. It was like there was a barrier between them, like he was looking at her through Perspex, but she'd just said, 'Is that it? Is that *all* of it?' And he'd lied and said yes, that was it, that was all. Carolyn turned to go, it seemed, but it was like something, a thought, had struck her. She said, 'You think you've got away with it, don't you?' Gamble felt his heart beating in his neck, and thought, ridiculously, about iambic pentameter. 'What?' he said. 'No, I don't. How could I? Of course I don't.' Carolyn – he remembers this clearly – squared up to him, like a boxer might, said, 'You were that girl's death sentence,' she said. 'You were. You're a malignancy, Greg. You're toxic.' Gamble remembers smelling the cloy of himself, of seeing her mind work, right there in front of him. Carolyn stepped closer to him, too close, but he didn't move. She said, 'You know, everyone thinks you're just a benign little man going about your everyday business.' He could smell the breath of her by then. 'But you're a dangerous, pernicious bastard.'

There was nothing he could think of to say, he'll say he deserved all that, and more, but Carolyn watched him, struggling, as he was, to find a reaction. When it was clear that he couldn't, she shook her head before she left him standing in the darkness. 'You always were a complete fucking shit, Greg.' And then, 'I wish it had been you. I wish it was you that was fucking dead.' She said it out of the corner of her mouth, so as not to wake Isabelle, he thought.

Perhaps he was thinking of this as he ran across the road to his house from the Old Doll Factory. Perhaps it seemed like four years ago was only yesterday to him. But the front door was open, and that surprised him. Carolyn was upstairs with Isabelle. He could hear them talking. He'll say it was like listening to cats, purring. By the time he'd made himself a cup of tea, Carolyn had come downstairs, alone. She placed the stolen lipstick on the work top as if it was some kind of award.

'I've grounded her,' she said. 'In case you're interested.'

Gamble nodded; he knew he had to. He'll say he felt then that the girl from the building opposite had implanted herself into him. Her imperfect face was in his head, and when he looked at Carolyn, it was as if he was watching a transformation from young to old before his eyes. By comparison, Carolyn's face was sagging from plumpness and age, he thought. He looked at her mouth, a perfect mouth in its own way, but the lips were thin, the lipstick dried into darkish clumps at the corners. He thought she might have done something with her eyebrows, but couldn't work out what. He'd been teaching Shakespeare to his year tens, and he'll tell how the line *'My mistress' eyes are nothing like the sun; Coral is far more red than her lips' red'* was floating about his head.

'Yes.' It was all he could think of to say, and he sighed. His face was smarting with, what? – guilt? Embarrassment? He took off his glasses, and for something to do, started cleaning them with the corner of his shirt. The fact of the scratch he felt irritated by. Carolyn tutted. She did what seemed to be an uncertain little dance. It was, Gamble realised, a performance, a demonstration of frustration – in him.

'Christ,' she said, at last. 'Leave it all to me, why don't you?'

And Gamble wondered whether that was passion he was seeing, or volatility. Either way, it made him nervous, and he called her name, but only weakly, as she headed back upstairs. She didn't stop.

Sitting by himself, with the house completely quiet, he twisted the lipstick about with his fingers on the table, and he let his thoughts work. You should yearn for a child, not end up with one, is what he was thinking. You should be prepared to love it. You should be ready. He thought back to Carolyn telling him she was pregnant. She'd missed a pill, or something. It wasn't joyful. And he thought, you don't think of a child as a person, you think of it as a belonging, a possession, an emblem – all different things, he knew, but his thoughts were running away with him. Being a parent, he thought then, is more than just biology, that's reductionist in the extreme to think that. But, he was thinking, it's not miraculous or magical or a triumph or even a particularly clever thing to do. You're not you any more for a start, is what he was thinking.

You're a *father*. You're someone's *dad*. And that makes you feel different about yourself. You deviate from yourself – your self, that is. You start fearing things you didn't before: motorways, electricity, news, air, water. You try to develop mantras, parental tics: 'isn't she lovely?' 'don't do that, sweetheart,' 'daddy's girl,' 'whoopsadaisy.' You dread killing the child, accidentally, or on purpose. You can't take your eye off them. You can't ever be off duty. Never. You dread them growing up as failures or mental cases or drug addicts or criminals. You start comparing your kid with others and wondering why yours is slower at walking, talking, at algebra or ballet or creative thought. You start laying the blame elsewhere – anywhere else – but really, you know it's all your fault, your genetics, the examples of parenthood you follow. And the disappointment is something no-one ever tells you about. You yearn for the child to develop some independence, and when they do, it scares you half to death. You watch them grow and change, and instead of counting their birthdays, all you count is your own, and you see your own life sliding away. And then there's your wife. She becomes a mother. Your mother. You might even call her 'mum', or worse, 'mummy'. You look at her body and see how it's changed. You listen to her voice and hear a mother's. You hope to God you don't sound like a father. Everything is routine and planned when you have a child. Everything. Your wife says, 'We won't let the child rule our lives. After all, it wasn't planned.' And then the child is born, and rules your life completely. There's an initial flurry of interest in the child, and you spend some time showing her off to family and friends and work colleagues, but the resentment at the sudden lack of impulsiveness is painful, and the lack of sleep is a torture. You look at other women, who, ironically see you as intensely virile and suddenly ragingly attractive, it seems. You think, they know what's going on in my life, they know how much it's changed, maybe they understand me. Women talk to you who wouldn't have given you a second look before. But, look, you're still a man with needs, only now, there's no fucking chance, even if you found your wife attractive. You can't help wondering if there are chances elsewhere. Just some relief. You ask yourself if you're *really* so faithful. You feel off the rails, cast out, emasculated, but you're supposed to feel like a man, a hero, a protector. You find yourself not in the least bit interested in the child. Where, you ask yourself, is this unconditional love they told you about? You hope it comes to you at some point, but when – if – it does, it creeps up on you disguised as responsibility. Of course, you cannot *say* any of this. You must keep it parcelled up and secure. It must never be said, or passed on. Ever. You cannot say a thing. Saying it would make it real. You must only express gratitude and pride. You must do this, even if you know it will breed contempt and an even greater capacity to lie (to act the part, some might say). But that doesn't stop it pulsing inside you. Everything you think and feel from the moment the child is born – from before then, actually – is propelled by fierce gusts of gratitude. And there grows an aggressive need to find who you think you ought to have been. You think sometimes you're being obtuse, perverse or ungrateful, after all, your child is perfect. *Perfect.* What if you'd had one with imperfections? Imagine that. You wanted – still want – your life to be a beautiful piece of art, on a canvas or a musical score, or gorgeous words on a page, don't you? Well, when you realise you can't have that, you wish it on your child. Which, really, is the most destructive of things to inflict on your own blood. But it's the most gratifying.

This, all of this, Gamble will tell you. He'll say he's being honest, that this was what he was thinking about there in his kitchen. When he looked at the time, it was way past midnight. He fingered the lipstick. He clicked it open and smelt it. It made him think, even more, about the girl opposite. He thought of her, and he saw a small animal, or a small, perfectly formed flower he couldn't quite get a proper picture of. The more he thought about it, about her, the more he adjusted the way he viewed that. When he thinks about it now, he'll say maybe he was thinking of an orchid. He smelt the lipstick again, and he replayed the scene in her flat. He was, he knew, being propelled towards something. He thought about the conversation they might have had. He'd have asked her about that thing he'd seen: her being slapped on the side of the road. He'd have asked her about that. He'd have asked who the man with the baseball cap was, the one with the tattooed script on his arm – the thug – he's sure he would have. He'd have asked her a lot of things. And she would have trusted him. She would have responded. She would have made him feel like a man, like a hero, like a protector. He wanted to know her, know her name, know things about her. And just thinking this, he felt a levelling, a calm, a peace, settle over him like a seventh veil.

He decided to lie down in the spare room. He thought it was for the best. He left the lipstick on the table, but he was to come downstairs only a couple of hours later to collect it, to keep it next to the bed. He'll say he's not sure why he did that.

Isabelle had begun sitting, offhand, watchful, next to him in the car on the way to school each day. It was as if she was waiting for something to happen, like she was preparing herself and her head was turned away like she was just gazing out of the side window. Gamble will look back and think she seemed to have quietened her breathing, even, so as to be less conspicuous to him. About a week after the lipstick incident, something happened. That morning, as soon as they arrived at school, as soon as Gamble had parked up, she was out of the car mumbling something about catching the bus home later, that she wouldn't need a lift, and she disappeared herself in a menagerie of year elevens. He'll say he thought she looked pale, washed out. He watched her until he lost sight of her, and an Irving Layton poem sprang into his mind, something about a lovely daughter, or a foolish one, he couldn't quite remember the words. Poetry, he thought, as he sat in his car, was something he was using to deal with the climate change in this relationship with her, and a lot of other things. Poetry, words, he thought, were his salve.

It was getting towards the end of the autumn term and, as usual, things were slowing down and quickening up at the same time. As the years had worn on, he had come to dread the holidays – the long summer break was bad enough, but even Christmas (especially Christmas, to him) was a discomfort. They'd seemed to come round more and more quickly, school holidays, and, year on year, the prospect of spending time at home grew more and more awful. This year, though, he felt bloated with the idea of getting away from work, of moving towards a different part of himself. The thought of it raised his spirits, so he actually felt floaty, a little light-headed with it all.

It was his duty day. The canteen at break-time, making sure students didn't kill each other in the rush at break-time, and patrolling the corridors at the beginning of lunch, but he didn't see Isabelle during the day, at all. He'll say that wasn't unusual, particularly, though he'll admit he wasn't really looking for her. His lessons, he felt, went well. He was on the ball, engaging, smart, quick-witted, sometimes even comedic and swaggering, he thought. He thought some of his pupils might have even admired him. Something about the day energised him. There was a sense of him being unstoppable, even his aches and pains – and they were more than that by then – were easier to deal with. When the last lesson finished and all pupils had gone, he decided against taking his painkillers, thinking he felt good enough, that he could cope, and didn't need the help that day. There was marking to do, and he decided he'd do it at school, then, on the way home, he'd stop off at that shop and buy a bottle or two of red, flirt a little with the ex-student behind the counter there. He continued to have blurry thoughts about the girl from the building, and found himself strengthened by the fact of them. He wanted to whistle, listen to music, and, yes, write some poetry. In the staff room, he made himself a cup of coffee, but had to use someone else's mug. Wherever his had gone, he didn't know. Uninhabited, the staff room was an unearthly place, an echo chamber of past chat. The English teachers had a corner of huddled chairs, some stacked with novels and play texts, near the window, and there were biscuits, always half-empty packs, on a low table. There was a disordered beauty about that, he thought, and he sat with a few exercise books on his lap and sighed, but it was a different type of sigh. It was almost contentment. His mind was full of possibility just then, and it seemed to him that he'd perhaps made everything over-complicated, and that, actually, things were simpler than he'd been making it. He felt as if he could be surfacing from deep water.

He really thought he could be. He straightened his back and felt it click into place. Outside, it was dark already, and when he stretched like that, he caught sight of himself reflected back at him from the window pane. He noticed a smudge, a stain, on the pocket of his shirt, and when he looked down, there was a growing labyrinth of red where his pen had leaked. He stood up, too quickly, snatched the pen out of his pocket, and the exercise books slipped off his lap, and then the table wobbled, and the coffee mug upturned, and the biscuits fell onto the floor. He was saying something like, 'Oh shit,' and 'Fuck it,' when Miss Henshaw swept in.

'Mr. Gamble,' she said. 'Greg. I'm glad I've found you.'

And he was standing, instantly feeling like he'd just been accused of something. The impulse to apologise – always there – overtook him, but she brushed it away. She was walking towards him, saying something he wasn't processing, only catching the end of a sentence, the fact of her wearing high-heeled shoes, and then the look on her face.

'Sorry,' he said, meaning about the mess, the coffee, and the biscuits, he noticed then, all over the floor.

'Oh, look, no need for you to apologise. I've got Isabelle in my office now,' she said. Despite what she was saying, she had a look on her face, a manner, that made Gamble feel at once shrunken and swollen, and he couldn't work out if she did it on purpose. Automatically, he placed his hand across the stain on his shirt, but she had turned on her high heels, and Gamble followed her, mechanically, trying to keep in step.

Isabelle was sitting in the office with her hands draped across the armrests of an easy chair. It wasn't the obvious choice of position for a child who was in trouble, although, as soon as Gamble saw her, he'll tell you he had the impression that she could – and would – have sprung away if there had been a clear escape route. Miss Henshaw said, 'Sit down, Greg,' and when he did, Isabelle crossed her legs away from him and sighed, and he realised that was how he must sound, all the time, at home.

'Now,' she said. 'Isabelle has something to say to you.'

Isabelle folded her arms, turned her head away from Gamble. The back of her head, he noticed, had the exact same flare from the crown as Carolyn's had.

Gamble will say it was as if he, they, the three of them, were all parcelled up, sealed up, in a vacuum of silence just then. He knew better than to try and break it. And the three of them sat like that as if trying to second-guess each other. There were a number of filing cabinets – maybe four – grey, and he couldn't help wondering if there was a file with his details in it, and what it might say about parental complaints, absences. He'd thought there must have been a draught from somewhere because the tips of tissues, poking out of a box on the desk kept trying to flutter, and so did some paperwork. Something on the other side of the window flickered and a chill was making the hairs on his arms stand up. Isabelle, he noticed, started rubbing the tip of her index finger against her thumb as if she was rolling something around. He'll say the light in the room was almost painful to him, yet Isabelle sat, her eyes enlarged, edged with aggression. Eventually, she said, 'It wasn't my fault.' The way she'd said it sounded self-possessed and he'll say the look on her face made her seem like she was preparing to be a human sacrifice. He knew he should be reacting in a particular way, like a father would, but he couldn't arrange his thoughts into that just then, he couldn't think how to be that.

'Well, now, Isabelle.' Miss Henshaw leaned forward, clasped her hands across the fluttering paperwork. It was a practised move, Gamble thought. 'You know what appropriate and inappropriate behaviour means, don't you?' she said.

Isabelle sniffed, coughed, and to Gamble, it sounded an odd thing to do. Though she wasn't looking at him, Gamble will say he was sure she was trying to make herself cry. He realised she'd been picking at the sleeve of her cardigan and it was ragged. He thought about the word 'inappropriate' and how insubstantial he'd always considered it.

'Don't get upset now,' Miss Henshaw said. 'But, punching another pupil is inappropriate, isn't it?'

'What?' Gamble knew he should have leapt up from his chair, but didn't. 'Punching?'

As he spoke, a spray of spit formed an arc out of his mouth and landed on the desk. Everybody saw it.

'On the bus, yes.' Miss Henshaw was grave, or acting the part of grave, very well. 'A year nine.'

'Isabelle,' Gamble said. 'What were you thinking? I mean, what happened? What's happening to you? A year nine? I mean . . .'

Isabelle had mustered some tears by then and was wiping her nose with the back of her hand, was snorting, antagonised. Seeing her like that, and knowing she'd forced herself to cry, he'd tell you, made him feel annoyed. He wanted to slap her face, and for a moment he understood what drove people to violence.

'She's already grounded.' He said this as if delivering a blow to the entire room.

'Dad, don't.' Isabelle sprang into life.

'For shoplifting.' Gamble will tell you, he wanted to, what?

– to punish her by telling all? 'For *stealing*,' he said, and he sat back, nodded slowly. He'll say now, that he felt a sense of malicious entitlement.

Miss Henshaw, though, seemed to be letting the information bounce off her, he thought, another practised move. She placed her hands flat on the desk as if business was done, as if too much information had been given, and both she and Gamble spoke at the same time, both of them saying it was probably time to leave and go home, sort it out.

Isabelle got up to leave, seemed to glance at the stain on Gamble's shirt, and he saw a flicker of, what? – contempt? He'll say she looked exhausted, agitated. She was trembling, he remembers. And that made him feel something hot underneath his skin.

Hannah had flickered, like an illness, a virus that flared every now and then. Her absence – he might admit, now, made worse by the mere existence of the canal – gave her a persistence. His thoughts teetered between ridiculous hope and fear. Physically at least, she had gone, but the thought of her had not. He saw her always in the present tense. She'd left this footprint in him, and sometimes Gamble wondered if it would ever really fade, and if he really was responsible, whether it was all his fault. At times, he could picture her clearly: her face, her neck. It was gradual when she started to fade, like a slow death, and then she'd come back to him, in his dreams – just the back of her head, or the crook of her collarbone, or her feet moving quickly, unstable. He thought she'd never be completely gone from him. She was like the sound of a dog barking in the distance in the middle of the night – you don't know if you're imagining it or not, and you give a name to the sound you think you hear because it's a comfort to think you know what it is. Sometimes, a few years ago, at night especially, he wanted to summon her, despite everything. And when he dreamed of her, her footsteps were quick, down by the canal. They were quick. Light. Feet, bare, rain-wet, mud-wet, and they slipped in the sludge. And there were rats down there, by the canal. Always rats. You could see where they'd gnawed at ropes and branches. You could see their imprint in the mud. See where they'd scampered. But her footsteps, they were quick. On and quickly on, past the boats behind the Bonded Warehouse. People lived there, didn't they? People maybe lived there. Aboard the boats. There were sounds. Coughs of sounds, anyway. And the sky, a forever of grey, shimmered in the raw water of the canal. And alongside the water, hands were stung by nettles, knuckles of hands, stung. And on, past the weir, on, into the woods, shadows clinging to the thick, dense cold of it, the thick, dense cold of the outline of the two of them, the two people, blurred outlines of the two of them. In amongst the oaks and silver birches, they stood. Face to face. It was if he was looking at himself and Hannah, both of them, from a distance. There he was, a man stooped – a tall man – his shoulders wide, hunched. His hair blue-black, or seemed to be in that dream-light. There was something crooked about his face, the profile of his face. An unevenness. A chin out of line. A nose not broken, but not straight. It was him, but it wasn't. And he stood, this man, his feet set, too far apart, legs bent but only slightly. And she, Hannah, her back, against the slant of a tree, both arms loose and hanging. The man's hands, the knuckles of his hands especially, were visible as he reached out to her face. Some wiry branches periodically obscured the view but it was easy for Gamble to work out the feel of fingertips against cheeks, lips, neck. Hannah didn't flinch. She did not. And her eyes, wide eyes that didn't blink, eyes wetted, that gazed through the man. And something was said. Something about a promise, broken, or not to be broken. A voice cutting through like a terror of calm, like the oncoming buzz of a fly. And the man looked away, downwards, made as if to move, as if to walk away, but Hannah stepped forward, her legs bare, first the foot, then the knee, then the thigh, and the flesh seemed grotesquely pale, dirty pale. And the man looked, saw, must have seen. And just for a split second, it was as if he would embrace her. Embrace her, or hold her, or choke her. Shake, or suffocate her, or push her. But he shook his head. That's what he did. He shook his head and turned and walked back towards the canal. Hannah didn't move, except the eyes, wide eyes that flickered downwards without blinking, and she moved her arms. Machine-like movements. The flesh of her whiter than it could possibly be. Whiter than powder, whiter than frost. And maybe she was waving. And the footsteps were quick, down to the canal. Quick. Light. Feet, bare and blue with cold, rain-wet, mud-wet, they were slipping in the sludge and the oil and the puddles of water. And there was skin being stung by nettles. Young skin. Young hands. And Hannah stood for a while, only a short while, the long coat open, the flesh beneath blueing with cold, looking with wide, unblinking eyes at the horizontal images moving, only slightly, on the surface of the water. And the look on the face, hard to put into words. Not upset, not sad, not relief, not really. This figure that was Hannah, standing there by the canal, it was more like she'd been petrified by the air, and what they could have been had been stolen somehow. It was a disappearing. That's the only way to describe it. It was as if things – people, events, time – had just been disappeared, or hadn't even really happened.

And it happened fast, without any hesitation. There was no hesitation. Hannah did not hesitate. And the movement was sinuous, graceful. A slowish release. Arms outstretched, hands, palm up, fingers splayed. And the material of the dress moved, and Hannah's skin caught the air. And there was no sound in this dream. The canal made no sound. The water, greasy-black with things from the past and oil from the factories, and long tall tin cans and cigarette ends and weeds, and, and, and. The canal water, it made no sound. Not any that could be heard from a distance at any rate. And it wasn't beautiful. This makes it sound like it was beautiful, but it wasn't. It was quick. It was.

For a couple of years, Gamble regularly had this dream. He'll say now that all that was left of her was this fever-dream of his. And Carolyn, she never mentioned Hannah, not to him. He'll say he thought she must have been at peace with it.

He'll tell how they left Miss Henshaw's office, both of them, like prisoners being expelled, and in the car on the way back home, Isabelle was, at first, wary, tightly wound, like a creature waiting for something inevitable. Gamble found himself glancing at her hands and thinking about the forming of a fist, of punching. He'll say he wondered where that had come from, who had put that into her. But it set him at odds with himself, the way she continued to pick at her sleeves and roll the bits of fluff and tease them into tiny black specks. It irritated him. And the way they just weren't speaking, the two of them, it made the atmosphere, the car, the inside of it, thick with thought. He'll say he could see the outline of her head in his peripheral vision, looking tight with self-defence or pride, or that simmering self-possession she'd developed somehow, and, he'll say, he let himself examine what he was feeling. Because it occurred to him that there is something about being a passenger in a car. He'll say he was thinking something about how vulnerable that makes you, how much you must trust the driver. There is something about the gestural exactness of things, the co-ordination of the mechanics of it for the driver, and of how unclear-cut it must be for the passenger, especially a young one and especially when it's getting dark. He could, he thought, drive off the road and into a tree, or at least aim for one. He could swerve into the line of oncoming traffic, or he could shoot a red light. It would be terrifying, for a passenger. It would be edifying, though. And a passenger would be powerless. He'd slung his jacket on the back seat. He knew the pocket was within reach if he stretched, and he did. It meant he had to lean, awkwardly, through the gap between his seat and Isabelle's. He felt his breath bounce off her as he leaned across. At the same time, he accelerated, just a little, as if one movement had caused the other. With one hand, he scooped out his pack of cigarettes from his jacket pocket. Beside him, Isabelle was as good as passive, she didn't even flinch, and he couldn't work out how false that was. He saw she'd had her ear pierced. He saw the glint of an earring, a flower of some kind. He only saw that then. He didn't know she'd had that done, and that annoyed him. He glanced down at the dashboard, and, impulsively, he'll say now, watched his speed begin to increase. He shook the pack of cigarettes. It was intentional, that; he wanted, he'll say now, to incite something. When he took both hands off the wheel, he realised that was something he hadn't done in years – steer with his knees, that is – and that it was something

Carolyn hadn't liked him doing, back then. So, he made his movements – the selection of the cigarette from the pack, the placing of it in between his lips, the search for the lighter in his trouser pocket – deliberate, unemotional, complicated. The road ahead was clear, dark, rolling towards him – them – like a film reel. The spark from the lighter's flame set a bluishness about things, and he held it against the tip of the cigarette for longer than he needed to. In that light, he could see how unangelic Isabelle looked. He knew the speed was creeping up, and there was a junction approaching – this was his usual route home, he knew every bump, every pothole, every imperfection in the road, he'd driven it for years, too many years he'll say now. He inhaled smoke deeply, tar felt thick in his mouth, his throat. It had started to rain, but he didn't bother with the wipers, and outside was going past in small sparks. All of this was making him feel light-headed. He didn't slow down. Trees (were they oaks?) tapped past, butterfingered. And he became acutely, beautifully, aware of his surroundings, the outside, just then, already going past at fifty miles an hour, maybe more. Isabelle made a sound, a throaty one, and it might have been a cough – the car was filling with smoke. Up ahead, the whiteness and redness of the Stop sign. Gamble opened his window, and the rushing air made Isabelle gasp, he heard that. Everything was deliberate then, everything. He felt, he'll tell you, cruelly aware. He saw Isabelle splay her hand, then clutch the side of her seat, her sleeve tattered from picking. He actually saw her harden, saw her brace herself. One more drag on this cigarette, he thought. The pitch of the engine was a moaning, rising hum. There was a sense of him, of them, falling, headlong into air, or water. It was more than just speed. Just before he braked, he was thinking, misthinking, a line from that Irving Layton poem about deep grasses, and going faster, and catching a foolish daughter. And he was wondering if they'd stop in time, if the car would, if he'd be able to stop it, if he had anything to lose. It was like it wasn't part of him, this scene. To him, it was all pantomime. He remembers seeing the tips of his fingers, then his knuckles, tainted with blue as he held the steering wheel at last. He could see Isabelle's heart throbbing, the pulse of her, in her neck, or thought he could. He thought, briefly, what kind of man am I, exactly? And then he thought it didn't matter, because he *was* a man. He felt beneath all light just then. His movements were automatic, his feet that is, the way he moved them, the way he shifted his foot from the accelerator to the brake, the way he pushed the clutch. He only realised he was panting, like a runner does, when the car skewed sideways and pulled or jerked or skidded towards the verge, and it stopped. The wheel, the tyre, made a thud against the kerb, like an idea, or the punchline of a joke. He wanted to laugh, Gamble did. He could feel hysteria rising from low down. There was ash on his trousers. He didn't know where the cigarette had gone. Isabelle, he saw, might have been crying – properly. He didn't think he needed to say anything. Light, anyway, was leaking in, bisecting – dissecting – her face. And a lorry passed in front of them at the junction there, long, like a breath.

'We could have had an accident,' Isabelle said, but it wasn't her voice exactly.

And Gamble thought, you were the accident. He whispered it. He wasn't him any more. He'll say he didn't care if she heard or not.

They were home in ten minutes. Gamble drove the rest of the way carefully, or more carefully. And that was deliberate.

Doing the opposite, driving slowly, he knew, exacerbated the fact of the speed he had been doing; it disrupted the optical flow. He was being *careful*, making the *uncareful* much worse. He knew all this. There was a science to his thinking, he'll say now, as if being careful was an equal and opposite reaction, yes, but he wanted *specifically* to make it worse. For her. And Isabelle, he'll say, had been unnerved. She clung onto the side of the seat, she sniffed, he could see her profile, the angle of her neck, her jaw, the curl of her pierced ear, the fact of her staring ahead, trying, he'll say, to pre-empt his next move, to prepare herself. But, and this is how he'll describe it, it was as if a spark had arced across wires in his brain and he was playing a different game. He could feel himself decompressing. He had barely stopped the car outside his house, and Isabelle was out, like she was absconding. He watched her slip, lose grip, and almost fall in the slurry of damp leaves on the pavement, and at the time, he thought that was droll. To him, then, she looked insubstantial, like a child again. Carolyn, he could see, wasn't yet home, and he watched Isabelle fumble to get her key in the lock. The wind blew her hair into a wreath around her head. Her face was a mask. He watched her shift her weight from one foot to the other. He imagined she must have been shaking.

It was still raining, or felt like it was. He closed his eyes, sat, thinking about – experiencing, really – an urge to unstick himself from all of that: the street he lived in, the marriage, the job. Thoughts and words and ideas floated about like torn paper in his mind and he closed his eyes. He saw the rails he was on and wanted to not be on them any more. He wanted to lose the grip he had on that reality. When he opened his eyes, it had been his intention to go inside his house, to pack a bag and to leave. Go, where? – it didn't matter. He felt justified. He'd decide where he'd end up later. But she, the girl from the building opposite, he saw her, and she was walking towards him. She wasn't wearing a coat, and rain – he could see it was raining heavily by then – had dampened her clothes so that by the time she reached his car, she wore them like another skin. He leaned across, opened the passenger door, but she stooped and was blinking through rain to see him.

'Greg,' was all she said. She said his name. Just that. And in her hand she had a letter. The rain suddenly came down heavily, like it does sometimes, but he could see the letter was addressed to him, and the postmark was from the hospital. It was his letter. It must have fallen out of his pocket in her flat. Her hair was becoming darkened by rain, thicker, stuck to her head, and she seemed to back away. Gamble will say this, all this, reminded him of Hannah and he got out of his car, was bombarded by raindrops, and both he and the girl half-ran towards the Old Doll Factory and inside.

He'd followed the girl upstairs. They were running, or half-running, and he wanted to say something but didn't know what, and when she pushed open the door of her flat, he hesitated. She turned and stood still for a moment, like actors do when they're supposed to have been shot and want to make their death scene dramatic. He'll say he felt if he crossed the threshold into her flat then, it would have been important, decisive, and he'll say he thought he needed to be sure. He was right, he'll tell you now. The girl relaxed and walked towards the window of her flat, started looking out. All he could see of what she could see was a dense sheet of rain which had turned outside into nothing. She was still holding the letter, and perhaps it was that that made him go in. So he moved towards her, sat down on the sofa, slowly. He could see, or thought he could see her reflection through the rain, could see she was trying to smile. He adjusted himself in the seat as if he was about to engage in an arm wrestling competition. He tapped his foot.

'Thank you,' he said. And when she turned to him, he motioned with his head towards the letter she was holding.

'Ah, yes,' she said, and held it out to him like she'd forgotten she was holding it. 'It must have dropped out of your pocket the other night. Looks important. Hospital.'

'It's nothing,' he said, and he took it from her, turned it over in his hands. It was almost useless by then, he thought, drenched by rain, and crumpled.

'It looks important,' she said, again, and she sat down beside him. 'Hospital.'

Her eyes, what colour were they? He couldn't work it out. Some colour that looked like watery blue, or grey, really, liked washed out shirts.

The gas fire purred. It wasn't the only light in the room, but it cast a greenish glow, so the shape of her face was altered by shadows. It still surprised him, there being a gas fire there and he must have glanced over to it.

'Retro,' she said. The thought that she might be able to read his mind might have terrified him in other circumstances. Instead, though, he wished she would get wine from her kitchen. He wished they could start where they left off the other night. He felt himself running his fingers along his neck from his ear to his collar bone. He does that for comfort, but he saw her watching him do it, watching his hands. She'd sat beside him, and moved her legs up and beneath her. Bare legs, he saw. And clothes soaked to thin, clinging to her. She reached for the pack of cigarettes, lit one and floated back into the seat. The smoke she breathed out tasted hot to him, but cast blue as cold as ice into the room between them. His skin felt suddenly heavy, as if he was a performer wearing make-up. He wanted to say, 'Sweetheart.' He wanted to call her that then. He wanted to say, 'Sweetheart, I adore you.' He wanted to say something like that. And he was thinking about time being somewhere else because poetry was coming to him, coming at him, just then.

She breathed out more smoke in two thin lines from her nose. Then, she leaned towards him. The cigarette, between her fingers, looked like part of her, and she held it, placed it between his lips. He could feel her thumb resting on his chin, and he shuffled in the seat, sat closer to the edge, ready to spring away. But the smoke in his mouth didn't taste like smoke, it was nectar. It dawned on him that this, he thought, this is something I deserve. And he was thinking something about her fingers flicking away ash, because the poem in his head wouldn't leave him alone just then.

'Are you going to open it?' she said. The expression on her face, what was it? Hopefully blank? He was struggling to work out his own reaction to it, to her. Could he feel himself transforming? He didn't know. And into what exactly? 'The letter,' she said. She was, he'll say, close to, sturdy, oaky, not in the least bit passive, like a thief, he thought. Her tongue flickered behind those lips. To him, she didn't look real – he'll say, if anything she looked like a broken doll. Perhaps they both were just then, broken, that is.

He remembers he ran his hand through his hair because he'll say he needed a reason to hesitate, or, more likely he just felt self-conscious.

'You have a great face,' she said – something like that, he thought, or perhaps he wanted her to say that.

'Look,' he said. 'It's not simple here.'

He needed a cigarette and he reached for the pack. He glanced at her as if to ask, then took one, lit it with her matches. His hands were trembling and there was a huge pleasure in that, at the time.

'I have to ask this. I have to say it.' He coughed, or rather, cleared his throat. He breathed the smoke out sideways away from her. 'I can trust you, can't I?'

She squinted at him through the layers between them. Even at that moment, he couldn't bear the fact that she might somehow disappear – perhaps Hannah flickered into his thoughts – and he waved his hand through the smoke. He'll say now he was preparing to tell her what he thought, what he feared. He was on the verge of telling her all his anxieties. He'll say now he just needed someone to talk to.

'I'm sorry,' he said. 'I am, really. But, I mean, I have to ask.'

She stubbed out her cigarette into an ashtray that she'd placed on the armrest of the sofa. It was the flowing movement of someone without a need to care.

'You think you can't trust me?' she said. There was an expression she had which made her seem translucent, her neck, her shoulders, and he suddenly felt he might lose her, lose the thread of her if he didn't say the right thing.

'I don't even know your name.' He was a brave fool, he realised.

'Greg, look,' she said. 'Surely you wouldn't be here now if you thought you couldn't trust me.'

Her eyes glistened, her face was suddenly bony – no, it was sculpted out of stone. That, in itself, was a statement.

Everything about her said something like 'Yes, I know what you're thinking'.

And his thoughts were multiplying, like dreams do.

'I'm, I don't know, older than you,' he said. He wanted to be deferential but at the same time he wanted to chip away at her. 'Old enough to be your father.'

'You're not that old,' she said. 'And I'm not that young.'

Her hair, he wanted to touch it then, touch the drops of water on her shoulders. And her breath, he wanted to taste it. He was a savage, a cannibal. He wasn't embarrassed by that, then, and he wondered if that, his brazenness, was written all over his face.

'You look it,' he said. 'You look like you could still be at school.'

She smiled at that – half-smiled, anyway – and he clenched his hands into fists. She'd noticed his wedding ring, he saw that happen.

'Your daughter – it is your daughter, isn't it? She looks like you.' To him it sounded like a challenge, like an insult, more like, and he couldn't hide that. And she said, 'She does.'

'She was an accident,' he said. If you ask him now why he said that, he can't explain, except to say, at the time, he just didn't want to be known as a father. 'Not an active choice.'

She hesitated, and he wanted to grab her and stop the trajectory of this conversation. She lit herself another cigarette, said, 'I don't really know what you want me to say.'

She was looking at him, and it was like a hypnotic thing happening to him, so he didn't feel her reaching for his hand until she squeezed it.

'You can trust me,' she said, her breath trailing like a veil. 'You can. Of course you can.'

Her face lightened, yet aged. He thought she might have seemed pleased with herself. But he felt she'd put him at the centre of things, it was as if she'd placed him there, like an ornament. If it was a game she was playing, he thought, it had drifted back and forth, but it felt that from that moment on, from the moment she'd said that thing about trust, that everything, every act would be cleaner and easier to distinguish, details would be purer, sounds would become separate from each other and would be easier to make out and put back together in a different, better, order. He looked at her face, the lips, those eyes. The darkness of the room meant the pupils of her eyes were large. She was a cat. And from within her, he tried to make out a magnetic force. He fed on his own reflection there. He tried to think what she was thinking, tried to make it an instinct. He wouldn't stay with her, not then, not that night. It had to be right, he'd thought. And she'd have known that, too. She'd have known he'd go home that night, that he'd leave the possibility of himself there with her, that he'd dash across the road, back home. That's what Gamble will tell you.

If you look at the canal, it's like looking at some people, you can just tell there is a darkness trembling just beneath the surface there, being suppressed. There is a sense of complication. There's nothing benign about them. Gamble, for example, fears what he does not yet know, and his anxiety escapes in wefts. He has a fair amount of insight into himself, he'll say, yet he'll admit that facing the truth of it isn't easy. It is mostly the insight that's the issue, actually, because when you suspect, when you think you know something – some darkness or other might be shifting about inside you – but you try to ignore it, or replace it, or overlay it with other thoughts, other actions, then you're asking for trouble, aren't you?

She'd called to him, from the open window, as he was crossing the road towards his house, and he knew for sure then, and he'd liked that. He liked the fact that he thought he'd got it right. He'd left her flat, because he wouldn't stay with her, not then, not that night. That's what he was thinking. It had to be right, he thought. He wouldn't push it. And he'd left, coolly. There'd been no drama. He'd said he had to go. He'd been charming, he thought. He'd felt something and thought it was calm, his mind, that is, he'd felt it was calm. And she'd called to him, from the open window as he'd crossed the road away from her. She'd said, 'It's Mara. My name.' He'll say, as he stood there, rain spattering onto his face, his glasses, looking up at her, he'd liked it, hearing her say her name to him like that. And he'd let himself say it, had felt the name of her in his mouth. And when he looked up at her, something about the way the rain did things to the image of her made her look like a fantasy, or the subject of a painting, as if he should really be viewing her from a distance to be able to see her – really see her – properly. He had an urge; he wanted her to know him as a duende, as a lover. Poetry was all over him, and he was thinking, or trying to remember a quote from MacNeice about stopping time, about God stopping time.

But even that didn't stop him from thinking something base. Deep down, he wanted to blow her a kiss, call her 'babe', be her boy, swagger away. He really did. All this, though, he kept inside, and he stood and watched her arms, her hands, and her face retreat behind the closing window.

She was, he thought, perfect, for him, to him. He saw

beauty in the fact of her imperfection. What she had was not just a face, more than just an expression, it was a declaration of the very substance of her. He'll say he had a fleeting thought that perhaps women like her don't exist, except in the imagination of poets, or the sick. He had a stack of questions for her. He wanted to know everything about her, to work her out, to piece her together. He felt like he was on the verge of something with her, on the verge of a *real* conversation, of a real *connection*, that, had he been in his twenties, they would have started by a meeting at a party, say, and, let's say there'd have been a bottle of wine, maybe something to smoke – some *pot*, he'll say – then a talk about literature, a quiet corner away from everyone else, and then . . . he had the fantasy worked out. For now though, for then, all that, he'll say, he felt, awaited him. He was enjoying the germination of it all.

He thought, or tried to remember, but couldn't, quite, another MacNeice quote about time and life not being the same as before because she was there. He might have even said something like it, let the rain pitter into his mouth, on his lips, his tongue, like kisses.

Walking towards, and then into his house, though, was like walking into another universe. The mirror near the door was insolent. The man staring back at him from it looked like the sort of man to say something like: 'My wife', 'Mortgage' and 'Pension plan'. That kind of man. He stepped forward, examined the face of this man. The forehead, he noticed, had crinkled like the skin on the top of boiled milk. The hairline, was it receding? There was a stoop, a roundness, to the shoulders, and something going on with his neck – the skin there. And his eyes, they looked wary – more than that, actually – like someone shut in an unfamiliar room, in the dark.

And right there, he could see the deepest tracks of things; he could see the younger him, yes, but he could see Isabelle, too, underneath it all, the truculence of her, and yes, that uncarefulness of her. He sighed, of course, or tried to. He still held the letter. He'll say now, he was afraid of it, that letter. He placed it on the side there, on the shelf next to the door, next to where Carolyn had left a pile of bills that needed to be paid. Where he'd felt pangs of excitement in his chest only seconds before, now it was a distant stampede that he could feel, and he knew he was launching off into a different orbit. All around him was the imperceptible trail that was the life he'd made there. Ghosts, everywhere. He thought of the two of them, the three of them, living, as they had done, there: all the years, the Christmases and birthdays, and – Jesus – the anniversaries. He saw the rise of the stairs, and footsteps there, he could feel the movement of all of their bodies, he could hear the voices – the shouting, the whispering – and he could hear the crying. It wasn't all wounds and injuries, but there were scars he could make out, imprints. And they were all part of him, weren't they? He could feel his breath catching, like a snore, and he imagined inflammation, blockages, growths. His legs felt shaky, as if he'd been running, and he held onto a bookcase to keep upright. If Carolyn had been there she'd have said he was freaking out. And he thought about that as he felt himself leaning against the wall. He bore those words, the potential cruelty of them.

Think of someone – a man, like Gamble – diminishing, draining out, crumpling against his own reflection. Look at the beginnings of that bald spot at the back of the head – the hair is definitely going grey, it's wispy at the crown – and look at the way the flesh at the nape of the neck there is puckering against the collar of the shirt. Is he crying? He might be. You might feel something for him, sorry, perhaps. You might even think you *understand* him. You'd be missing things though, as he did. He couldn't see the wood for the trees.

In his kitchen, he sat, ten, maybe fifteen minutes later. He'd just about got out from under all that he was thinking and was lighting cigarettes, two, one right after the other, but quickly putting them out. It was because of Carolyn, that. He knew smoking in the house annoyed her, and anyway, the taste of them didn't seem right to him. It was like his body knew something before he did. His chest felt heavy, anyway, his heart did. He was settling though. His breath was calming, flattening out. There was, he'll say, a ridiculous darkness outside the window, through which he saw the reflection, this time, of Isabelle. She'd crept, like a ninja, he'll say now, downstairs and was standing at the kitchen door, watching him. There was a tangible sense of advancement about the way she moved and he could sense, rather than feel, her interest. He could, he'll say now, only think of something glib to say, like 'Can I help you?' or 'What?' But nothing he could think of seemed to be right.

She faltered. She was picking at the skin on her thumb and he could hear the sound of it clicking. He realised that was something he did and he looked at the state of his own fingers. Isabelle kept breathing as if she was about to speak. It was irritating him, that pause she did between breaths. In a rush, she said, 'You could have killed us.' And Gamble remembers feeling angry and saying nothing because of it. Isabelle waited. He'll say she seemed nervous, and at the time, he'll admit to liking that. She waited, then said, 'Where's mum? Do you know where she is?' And it was like a heavy door had been opened between them.

'No,' he said. 'I do not.'

He wanted to stand up, to pace around a little. He wanted to be a father just then, to take on the role of a father, but Isabelle turned to go.

'Young lady,' he said. Even he thought that sounded out of place. 'Isabelle. Get back here.'

Isabelle, though, did not stop. She continued walking away from him, and he, instinctively, followed her. They were half way down the hall when he put his hand on her shoulder. It was as if she'd been electrocuted, the way she reacted to his touch. She didn't even have to speak. Everything about her: her expression, her movement, everything said he'd lost her, that she despised him.

'Do not walk away from me,' he said. He didn't know what he was then. A father or a teacher, or a savage.

'Don't touch me,' she said. She really only whispered it, as if she was testing out the words to see if they would work.

'I beg your pardon,' he said, and he felt himself squaring up to her, like he'd felt Carolyn do to him. Now, when he thinks back, he'll tell you he felt like he was floating above the situation very slightly. He wasn't seeing her as his daughter, she was, then, an *issue*, a *sleight*.

'You heard me,' she said. And she looked at him, she glared at him, at one eye, then the other. She'd been wearing eyeliner, he could see it smudged. There was something different about the way she looked, the way her face was - not the expression, he could work out what that meant, no, there was something she was doing with her eyes. She was still wearing her school uniform, and that felt bizarre to him. It was like he was chastising one of his pupils, one he didn't know and didn't like. But it seemed to him then that they must both have held similar feelings for each other, and for a split second, there was a comfort in that. It was, he'll say, like he'd lost her, or let her go. He wondered what he'd have to lose if he was to slap her, and the image of Mara – yes, he could put a name to her now – falling as if through a trap door on the side of the road took him aback momentarily. There was a perfect twist in the confidence about Isabelle's lips – it was something she'd picked up from Carolyn – and he thought she was about to say something, so what he did next, he'll say, was because of all that. He said, he *whispered*, 'You, Isabelle, were an ugly, terrible mistake. The sooner you leave, the better my life will be.'

What Gamble remembers is that Isabelle reared back away from him. It was like he'd slapped her, but better than that. He knew he'd said it with a smile on his face, or on his lips at least. The sound of her footsteps on the carpet up the stairs behind him were so quick, it was like an animal escaping.

Gamble stood – he remembers this – for a while, feeling his strength increase. When he turned and looked at the man in the mirror, it was a different one he saw, one that said, 'Fuck this.'

There is a dream Gamble has, even now, maybe especially now. In it, he is remarkably, uncharacteristically, frank. He's talking to Mara. He says: 'I'm interested in you. Not you, perhaps, but what you say, or what you don't say, rather. You talk like someone has crossed out the middle bits. It's the gaps in what you say. You're out of reach, just. I like that.' He reminds her that he's married, of who he is, of who he is. *Who* he is. He tells her, obliquely, he might have 'issues', and that she mustn't call him, or text him, but she must be there for him and that he might have to disappear sometimes. In his dream, he gets the feeling, as clear and different and exciting as if he's just stepped into a different existence – more than that – as if he's been cast out to sea and is being buffeted by only slightly choppy waters, that this is the path he's on, like it or not. In this dream, he's good at deception analysis, but, even he will say, there is nerve in everything he says. She's enjoying this, he thinks, because he likes what he doesn't yet know. She feels like water in his hands, and he knows he has to keep catching the drips of her in his palms. And he talks to her with these wet hands of his. And what he says sounds up, jovial, spotless. He identifies with her, smears a layer of kindness over it all. And, to him, he'll tell you, it feels like a purge.

Gamble spent the weekend – the entire weekend – making a project of the girl, of Mara. He'll tell how he found he felt contemplative, and that each time he thought of her, it was with more and more precision. When he thought of her, when he summoned her to him, she swung towards him and let her language overlap his, let his overlap hers. In this imaginary, fantasy world of his, he was amazed at how quickly he found a connection with her. To him, it felt and sounded like fate – he'll say exactly that: how fateful it was that he was on the side of the road that time, that he saw what he saw, and that later, she was there for him, and helped him so openly. He felt his ego growing and hardening. He felt he was an expert at using and manipulating language to stroke this girl. Words, he thought, are not cheap at all. In the meantime, she, the girl, Mara, she seemed to keep her distance – the entire weekend, he didn't see her. The venetian blinds remained closed. But that was compelling, he thought, it surely would be, for both of them, and this communication, this *connection*, they'd started, the longer it took, the more he thought of her, the cleverer he knew she was. On Sunday evening, he stood at the window in his spare room. 'Talk to me,' he said, out loud. 'Tell me things.' He was talking through a glass pane, and he could see his breath on it, not quite obscuring the building opposite. But it was like she'd drawn him to her, already. It happens like that sometimes with some types of people. Needy, damaged types. And he felt like she was already his secret. Like she was part of his need then – part of the remedy for him. He was fighting clichés: the faster beat of his heart, the prickles of his skin, the flush, or, no, the tremor of, what, an urge or a retch. It was becoming delicious. He felt the taste of her on his tongue and in the back of his throat – or rather, he felt what he wanted it to be – and it was like syrup, or a serum, or a salve. It was all going so well, he felt swept along, high. Even when he heard Carolyn leave the house – especially then – he still felt strengthened. But, late Sunday, there was a pause, a lapse, a difference. The venetian blinds were being moved. At first, he thought he'd imagined it. And, as if someone had walked into his room and chastised him, he saw that it wasn't Mara struggling with the cord or the chain or whatever it was, it was a man, wearing his baseball cap sidewards. A skinny man, with a shirt, open. He could see that through the opening slats. And he could see Mara approaching this skinny man, from behind, slipping herself around him, her face – he could see it. He could make out the angle of her shoulders, the bareness of them. He'll say he felt like he was falling off a cliff, like he'd been nudged. He needed an exclamation mark. Something. Not this, not that. And the thought cupped itself around itself and he felt raw, exposed. He saw the line of blue script on the arm of the man. He felt disgusted, stupid, lonely. And he sat – fell – back onto the single bed as if he'd been shot.

He could hear music coming from Isabelle's room, and it was as if he was listening to it underwater, or from a different plain, and he wanted to go in and shout at her, to take this all out on her, to blame her for all this.

He'll say he didn't. He'll say he just went for a walk.

There was light enough to see along the towpath, some of it reddish and flickering from the opposite factories. Clods of sodden earth lined the way, and at intervals, torn out pages of damp pornography lay like musical vamps. He'll say he stopped, picked up a page or two, surprised that those types of magazines still existed, wondered if he might have been imagining them. He'll tell how it seemed he could easily make out the vestiges of frustration in every print, and the taunts, the conditioned passivity. Fragile bodies, it seemed to him, had been caught up in all that vastness down there alongside the canal. The faces of the women on the pages – he was sure he could see it – had been told how to look; there seemed no depth of truth in any of them. It was, he thought, as though the photographer had no intuition, and the women had no choice. There was such a sense of ceaseless doomed need about them, the women, their faces. Caged birds, he was thinking. That they would disintegrate alongside all that concrete and decay was, he thought, perhaps part of the process of it all. Alongside, there were petals, having fallen from something wild in the hedgerow. It was like confetti. And it seemed to Gamble that they, the flowers, and the women in the images, had been demolished, as if someone was trying to prove a point. She loves you not. The fact of all this being there made him feel naked, sluggish, as if he was walking in an invented world, as if he was a character in a film, or a novel or a poem; he felt underdeveloped, limp. Beside him, the water was a broken mirror, though he didn't know why it looked like that. It was beset with problems, the water then, and he was conscious of the dissatisfaction of it, of its inability to speak, of things that must be left unsaid, the sense that it was full of dangers. His reflection was drawn briefly into the water, absorbed into the shattered glass of it, bits of him repeated, but not all. He was, he knew, about to pass by the back of the Old Doll Factory, partially obscured, as it was, by trees, and smothered, it seemed, in ivy. He felt his legs thicken, his footfalls become heavier. It crossed his mind that he was only one of many whose imprints were in that mud there, or whose shoulder or elbow had glanced another's just there, by accident, or on purpose. He walked on for a bit, getting colder – too cold – and more agitated. The Old Doll Factory, as he passed it, had seemed, he thought, to jump out at him, like a joke. But it was probably because of the backdrop there was then, of those layers of early night, cyanosed into blue. Gamble will tell how he felt it all like a fearsome tiredness, an exhaustion. His head, he'll tell you, started pounding, and his chest hurt, and there was that nagging pain in his groin, or somewhere there. He couldn't tell where the pain was coming from, but it was like a prophecy.

He took himself home. He didn't even walk that far.

It seemed to him that days passed, they slid past. The nights were drawing in, there were Christmas lights up outside other people's houses. There was nothing soothing about the power of that. Often, when he was driving back home from work, the sky was astonishing, but he was less aware of all that than what was going on inside him, of course. He could feel his life leaking away into the suit he was wearing. Mara, the thought of her flickered; no, more than that, blazed, and she came to him, she materialised, he seemed unable to stop that from happening; he couldn't unthink her.

Carolyn, it seemed to him, had been keeping out of his way, or ignoring him, so when he arrived home and both she and Isabelle were sitting in the kitchen, it felt wrong, somehow, to see them both there like that. He remembers the conversation they were having seemed to stop, mid-sentence, as he approached them. Between him and them, there was a greater distance, of course, and he'll say he wondered if he should try harder to tune in to them. Neither looked at him, and he noticed Carolyn, thought she might have lost some weight, perhaps, or was wearing something he hadn't seen her in before. Isabelle's face, set into sullen, looked pale, and there was a high-pitched buzz coming from somewhere – something electrical, he guessed, or the boiler – which was like the sound of an oncoming fly or the start of a screaming migraine – it was almost spiritual. He thought, Isabelle's told Carolyn about that time in the car, and he braced himself. He thought, I'll deny it, it'll be her word against mine, I'll call her a liar. He heard himself swallow. Isabelle wasn't even looking at him. He'll say that when Carolyn inhaled, it was precise, as if she was an icon of the inner breath. She said, 'Isabelle doesn't think she should be grounded any more.' She pursed her lips, squinted at Gamble. They were playing at parents, he'll say now. He'll say he thought she was playing the 'good' parent, and he configured himself, or tried to, into a father. He said, 'Hmmm,' in an out-breath, unsure of the details of fatherhood. He had to try and get outside of himself, to make himself present. None of this was coming naturally to him. He glanced about the kitchen, which seemed to him to have been recently cleaned. All the work tops were so clear, it felt as if things had been moved or put away. He leaned back against the fridge, folded his arms so that he at least looked like the other two. His heart started beating as if he'd been running and he thought they must have been able to see the pulse of it all over him. He said, 'How long has it been?' and Isabelle said, 'Too long. A week. Ages.' And he didn't like the way she'd said it. Carolyn reached across, touched Isabelle's elbow. Gamble noticed her hands, Carolyn's, her fingernails, painted a soft pink, the intimacy of them and the way she was using them, and he didn't recognise that. He'll say he thought that was part of the process – the process he must have been going through, of distancing himself from these things. He thought that might have been normal.

He said, 'I don't think . . .' because he'd wanted to give himself authority, and time, to think. But Isabelle reared up in that way she could. It was as if there was an upsurge of energy inside her. When he thinks back to it, Gamble will say he felt like he'd detonated something in her. He felt like he needed to take cover. Carolyn said something to her, her name or something soothing, but Isabelle had leapt up. This was a controlled explosion, Gamble thought. He looked at the way she was moving. He'll say now she was like a machine, her arms like metal prongs. She uncoiled, physically. She clicked, her joints did. He thought he could actually feel the pressure waves from her. He remembers the shock of the shape of her. God, he thought, she's a woman now. When did that happen? Her T-shirt, he noticed, was short and it rode up. He could see her ribs, the tautness of the skin, her belly button, stretched to a startled 'O', the angle of her hips. Mara flared across his mind and he had to steady himself by holding onto the worktop. Isabelle wasn't even shouting, he remembers that, but he can't remember exactly what it was she was saying, except when she told them both, him and Carolyn, to fuck off. That was like the sound of bits and pieces of debris collapsing. In her rush to leave, the chair fell backwards, and both he and Carolyn looked at it lying there, upturned. He'll say he could feel the heat that Isabelle had left behind, and he expected Carolyn also could. Eventually, she, Carolyn, said, 'You don't think what?' and she'd looked at him in a way he didn't, or couldn't, recognise.

'I was going to say I don't think a week is long enough for, you know, what she's done.' He put the chair back upright, sat on it, so he and Carolyn were sitting close. He could smell her perfume, but it wasn't her usual, it was something stronger, heavier. He wanted to feel something, but couldn't. He wanted to feel a link, a union, a join to her. He tried, but all there was was this peculiar silence. He was thinking, maybe everyone feels like this, after a certain amount of time. He was thinking, perhaps it's all an inevitability. He wondered if what he was thinking about Mara would burn out, or if he could blow it out, but he didn't want to, really. He was thinking: I'm fifty-two, I'm not quite finished yet, everything still works, and I'm still alive, aren't I? He thought he could hear Isabelle's footsteps in her bedroom above them and glanced up to the ceiling as if he'd be able to somehow see through the Artex, the floorboards, the carpet, into her room. Carolyn, he caught sight of. She seemed to be looking for him in the same way he was looking for Isabelle. Her face was very full, very flushed.

'We've messed this up,' she said. A flat voice, like she was experimenting with the phrase.

And that was unusual. Gamble will say he felt a jolt of, what? Anxiety? Guilt? He'll say he thought she was reading his mind.

'What?' he said. 'You mean Isabelle? You mean with Isabelle doing all this?'

He waved his hand about his head like he was swatting a fly, or trying to. He wondered if he looked foolish doing that, so he covered his mouth with his hand. It was an unusual thing to do, he'll say now, all that movement, because it wasn't *him*, it wasn't what he would normally do. For a second, he thought she might reach across and snatch his hand away, see that his face had suddenly changed, transformed, and that his lip, his nose, had forked his face, that he had transformed, or deformed. Instead, she stood up. Looking back, he'll say it was like she was uncomfortable sitting so close to him.

Carolyn blinked, seemed to look at him, and he thought she surely must have been able to see Mara somewhere on his face.

'I mean, we've messed this up,' she said, and she looked around the room. She draped her hand across the worktop, and just that movement, that action, made Gamble feel full of sorrow. There was a sense that they were – she was – suddenly terrifyingly close to making some kind of declaration.

'Carolyn,' he said, or heard himself say. 'Look.'

He watched her jut out her jaw and knew her well enough to know she was grinding her teeth. The map of their life together was written all over her face. And he'll say now, he wanted to say something profound, or loving, or to tell her what he thought might be happening. It seemed like she was waiting for it. Like it was a test. Like she was holding her breath. But he couldn't. And instead, he just said, 'Look.' And he stood up and straight away he started to sweat and feel a bit sick. 'You know what I'm like.'

Even he, really, didn't know precisely what he meant by that. It was, he'll say, just something to say. Isabelle, or sounds that he thought might be her, filled the room. The clatter of footsteps matched thuds of pain he felt in his back, his thighs, his groin. It was like that for him more and more, and it was getting worse, he'll say now, it came on quickly. He pretended he was checking his fly, just for comfort, really, turned away from Carolyn.

'That's it, is it?' she said, and she was looking at her pink fingernails, anyway. 'That's all?'

She lifted her face, sniffed, and Gamble will say now that you could have mistaken her for someone who could hear some distant music that no-one else could. He looked at her neck, the skin there, stretching, and he couldn't remember kissing it, ever, instead his mind was emptying and filling at the same time, there were caged birds singing and petals, like confetti, having fallen from something wild in a hedgerow, and pearls, and orchids, and shattered reflections, and that seemed to be making it difficult for him to remember things.

And there was a moment, a gap, where one of them could have said something dramatic, or meaningful, or truthful, but it seemed to Gamble that Carolyn's eyes, she was doing something with them, and it didn't seem right to him, he couldn't work it out. He tried to want her, to trust her, he'll say that. And maybe there was an instant where he could have. But it passed. And she seemed to deflate in front of him.

He said, 'I don't really know what you want me to say. I really don't.' And he knew the words weren't his.

He'll say she looked like she was calculating something: the soft, frequent blinks, the slightly open mouth, the hardened eyebrows. She said something, but he can't remember now exactly what it was, something like, 'I think you probably do,' and she seemed, he says, to float away. And she seemed, he thought, to be capable of anything just then. And watching her walk away from him down the hallway, he says, was like watching her walk down a long slope – she looked like she was getting bigger the further away she moved, and he says he felt like he was getting smaller, but mushrooming, that it was a mushrooming feeling, he'll say, and he felt an odd beat to his heart. But it was when she turned. It was as if she'd put the brakes on. She was only half way down the hall, and she turned her head, her shoulders were round liked they'd been carved like that. She said, 'Let go now.'

He remembers that.

And he remembers watching her go, watching her open the front door and go. And he remembers hearing, rather than seeing, the flutter of paper, and knowing that letter of his, the one from the hospital, had slid onto the floor next to the shelf.

He had a shower. When he looked down at himself, naked, he saw he'd lost weight. He rubbed soap down his arm, across the shadow of a bruise and the little rash and the pinprick in the crook just there, across his abdomen, and turned to let the water spray across his face, his chest, his thighs. He was thinking, it isn't so much a pain, as a dull, dullish ache, and it was spreading from his groin now to his back. This was not constant. It wasn't a constant pain, and he consoled himself with that, but the feel of water against his skin there sent sparkles of irritation rather than calm. He knew if he touched himself – examined himself, let's say – exactly what he'd find, he'd felt it before, the little pearl of a lump. He knew, deep down, that there'd be no change, nothing would have disappeared, but still. He let his fingers glide over his hips and down and he tried to make his skin feel like someone else's, tried to navigate the creases and furrows as if there was only a biology to them, nothing else. He'll say he was doing it like someone who'd reluctantly promised to do something, like, say, attending your daughter's parents' evening. It was a duty. He'd read, on the internet, about how to use your thumb and fingers, how to roll your flesh and feel for things, and he was doing that. He did that. Of course, he'd done it many times before. And it was still there, it still was. A little pearl just beneath the surface of his skin, inside him. If he squeezed it, he could make it hurt, but he couldn't seem to make it go away. And he couldn't bear to look. He tried to think of himself as just a man in a shower, tried to see himself from outside of the cubicle. He saw one of his razors just there on the shelf next to the shampoo, and imagined the act of slicing through skin, or unsutured wounds. And he tried to think objectively, to imagine it was nothing, it was normal, for a man of his age, lumps and bumps, things like this. But he'd had a blood test, and the letter was downstairs, and he knew he was going to have to walk past it, again. And he knew, really, what the hospital would be telling him. Now, he'll say, he'll admit, that for an intelligent man, he was a fool. He sees that as insight. But he was thinking in metaphors. Terrible ones. Things about life being short, time running out, opportunities passing him by. And the feel of the water in the shower was claustrophobic, the heat of it. Everything felt out of his control, and being there under the force of that water made him feel like he was being thrust towards something, and he had no choice. There was shampoo, Carolyn's, on the little shelf in the shower cubicle they have. He squeezed some out into the palm of his hand, smelt it. He was sure it must have been expensive, but to him, it, or something in that shower cubicle, smelt of sour wine. He rubbed it onto his head, the shampoo. He felt his hands slip over the bones of his skull, and he thought about his brain, the workings of it, and he squinted his eyes closed when he felt some water run down his face. He'll say that's why his eyes were watering: because of the shampoo in them. That's what he'll say.

Later he sat in the spare room and read some poetry: W. S. Graham. He copied one out, by hand, and underlined the title, 'I Leave This at Your Ear'. Doing that made him feel unafraid, heroic – the act of writing, that is. Every now and then, he glanced outside, noticing the light in the window of Mara's flat across the way. He'll say it all felt carnal, like he should have been listening to jazz as he was doing it. He folded the paper and went and stood for a second outside Isabelle's bedroom. There was no sound, no light coming from the gap at the bottom of the door, and he imagined her in angry sleep. He ran his thumbnail along the crease of the paper he'd written on and thought the sound it made was like lips, parting, as if someone was about to speak. He thought about knocking at Isabelle's door, seeing if he could, maybe, put things right with her, or at least try to make things better, but when he really thought about it, he couldn't, not then. He tried to be quiet, he didn't want to wake her, as he walked away, down the stairs, and out of the house.

The Old Doll Factory leered down, but he'll say it didn't

seem to bother him, that. The door, he'll say, was closed – he still felt a fascination for that – and, one by one, he pressed each of the buzzers in turn. He'll say now, it was like watching someone else do it, press those buzzers. It was like he was watching someone from a long way off.

He'll tell how she'd answered – her voice had – and the sound of her had been metallic, he'd virtually seen it coming out of the tannoy at the door, it was an almost tangible thing, her voice, and when he'd said who he was, she'd come down, opened the door. And she was holding a cigarette between her fingers, she was smoking a cigarette, and for some reason, he was surprised about that. She didn't say anything, she just stepped to one side as if she'd been expecting him and he should go straight in, and he obeyed. As he passed her, he brushed her shoulder with his arm. She was, he remembers, wearing a dress with thin straps, blue, like she might have been expecting to go out somewhere. That, and the smell of her, the cigarette, her, he found comforting, sexy, even. It mixed with his fresh aftershave, like dirty with clean.

He'll say she followed him, that the door to her apartment was ajar, that they stood, unguarded, that he was unsure of what to say, so said, 'Hello, you.' It didn't sound like something he'd normally say, even to him. He remembers it sounded like there was an urgency, a whisper, as if he was recovering from a sore throat, or had been shouting, or crying, or that his voice was wearing out. Mara seemed to make herself smile, as if she hoped he would too. She was examining his whole face, standing there, and he knew, he could feel himself gazing at her, one eye, then the other he'll say now. He thought: what is it about her? He thought it might have been something to do with the light in there, a muted half-light that made her look wanton. He thought that was it. He doesn't remember how long they stood there, looking at each other – *into* each other – but he felt no embarrassment about memorising her, the very fine lines around her eyes, the tightness of worry or seriousness, he thought, across her forehead, and a sense that she hadn't slept much. And he wanted to touch her, just then. But he didn't. Instead, he rubbed a line from his own neck to his collarbone. She opened her mouth to say something, but it was just breath that came out, and he could smell it. To him, it was an electric smell, smoky, of course, but more industrial. He checked himself, just to see if he was feeling what he thought he was. He says he felt good then. Maybe not good, exactly, but some part of the identity of 'good'. He can't explain it. Not, quite. He was still gazing at her, one eye, then the other, and he felt – he liked – the suspense of it, the way there was something forming in it. But it still felt slippery, to him – she did, is what he'd say, like she felt as if she might be out of reach. It didn't feel right for him to speak, so he leant towards her, experimentally, placed his hands on her arms, let his face, his cheek, brush hers, but not the lips. Dirty with clean. Her skin, he'll say, seemed too smooth to be even human. Something and nothing. But he felt it, he'll tell how he felt something pass between them. Behind her, through a window, he'll say he saw the trees become still, become bluer, and she seemed to sigh, or there was something like the effect of a sigh, as if she was relieved. And he'll say he thought: Let go now. And that's when she spoke. And her voice carried through the brick and concrete, and twisted through the ivy, and outside along the surface of water. She said, 'You're shivering,' and she released herself from him and stooped to light the gas fire and the heat exploded, then fizzed, steady. She straightened to a stand, slowly, turned to face him. The smell of gas reminded him of his younger days, his student digs, briefly, and then it went, and the little bit of extra light there flickered, thrilling to him. His legs had weakened, and he sat down on her sofa and she looked down onto him in silence. The strange darkness felt to him like an obstacle between them. He'll say he saw her chest rising and falling faster than before and wanted to say something complimentary. He wanted to, but didn't. In one surprising, easy move, it seemed to him, she stood and pushed the straps of her dress off her shoulders and let it, the dress, fall. He'll say now that she seemed to move readily, like water. He took a long breath in – was it shock? – rested his head back.

'I don't,' he said. 'I'm not. Sure.'

He said it to the ceiling, and he could feel the workings of his own neck. The light, such as it was, the shadow, he knew, had caught the crease and furrow of his movement.

She smiled at him, but it wasn't a real smile, and he'll say how she stepped towards him so that the point of one of his knees touched her leg. He says he flinched, moved his head to one side, but not his leg. He'll say, though, that he could see her heartbeat in the flesh of her breasts, and her underwear, he thought, looked cheap, black.

She seemed to choose not to speak, but instead, to let their two bodies remain joined like a couple in a strange three-legged race. He'll describe how he was at odds with himself, and how she must have been able to see that, of how a thought seemed to hover above her, and how she appeared to him to wonder whether to act upon it, but he'll say he was teetering on the edge of it all.

'I know so little about you.' He'll say it came out like a purge.

'There's nothing much to know,' she said. And she must have realised her voice sounded silky.

He turned his head, at last, looked at her properly, knowing that the heat from the fire behind her had made her sweat because her skin had begun to glisten already, like that of a fish just beneath the surface of thin water, is the way he describes it.

'Tell me things,' he said, and he'll say now it was because he needed time.

He'll say the thought of her kneeling before him flashed into his mind and started playing itself out, but the blatancy of that made him shake the thought away. He'll say it was time he needed, just time.

'Go on,' he said. 'Tell me things, about you. Anything. I need to know who you are.'

He'll say he was stalling, holding back time, but he remembers her as being very compliant, standing there with most of her clothes off. He'll say it was as if she was being reprimanded, rightly. And she looked vulnerable, nicely vulnerable.

'I'm nobody,' she said. 'I'm just me, Mara. Nobody, really.' And she pushed her hair off her face, gave another of her smiles as if that was it, that was all.

He leant forward, looked up at her. There seemed excruciating pain coming from every line on his face, he could feel it. And there were pangs of doubt, of worry, springing from that.

'No,' he said. 'More.' And he felt her hands on the back of his head and it felt like a rush.

'My boyfriend,' she said, but her breath was catching against something, as if she was pulling back, he was sure of it.

What was it? Reluctance? 'He's, you know. He's not very . . .'

He was looking at her in the way that Carolyn did to him, and he stopped himself. He felt something like sympathy and it must have shown on his face, and it was clear she didn't like that.

'They call him Aitch, but that's not his name.' Her voice was breaking. 'He's not very . . .'

She hesitated, lost, it seemed, but Gamble said, 'More.' He mouthed it, like it shouldn't even have been said, and he meant it, he wanted to hear more. But she said, 'No more.' And she pulled his head towards her and he felt the skin of her abdomen against his face. It was almost unbearable. He nestled himself, his face, flat against her there and he felt a wetness from his own lips, like a kiss, but not. He had a tingling sensation, like a sickness, in his stomach he wasn't sure would ever disappear. It made him weaken against her and she seemed to know it, to feel it. And he'll say how he didn't have to push her very hard, and she – they – seemed to fall, so they were lying diagonally on the floor there, on the bare floorboards. In that light her body, he saw, was surprising. More like a child's than he'd thought it would be. His flesh, his neck, the collar of his shirt, he knew, would smell of washing powder and he wanted to hold her to him, to take it easy, but he'll say he did not, and he'll say his hand hovered, uncertain, above her breasts, then floated down onto her stomach and he felt the muscles there contract. And she reached, with one hand, each of the buttons of his shirt, pushing it open like, what? – she was unwrapping him? He watched her hands, and, he'll say, had a sudden fear that she would have expected more of him, more muscle, more hair. His ribs, he saw from above, were partitioned by blue light from the fire and he felt inadequate, unsubstantial, shy; he felt suddenly worried that if she should touch him, if she should dare to, she would feel what he had felt, that she would feel that little pearl-like lump, or worse, that he would infect her with something he had, but he felt like he couldn't stop then. He just couldn't. So when she touched his face, he'll say, she gave him permission and it seemed right for him to reach round and unhook, or try to unhook, her bra. But each time he tried, it remained fastened. She pressed herself against his chest, smelled at his skin – he could hear her breathing it in – and he felt his stomach flicker again, felt himself give. She whispered something too quiet for him to hear against him, and he could feel her reach round and trace the outline of his spine with the tips of her fingers. The feel of that released something in him, and he relaxed, and he felt, at last, it seemed to him, her bra spring unhooked and heard her clear her throat and breathe a sigh like a last breath. He dipped his face towards the top of her breasts – small, he'll say – and he brushed his lips against the skin just there as if she might be precious, and saying this makes him feel close to tears even now, but without admitting why. Heat from the gas fire, he knew, was rippling the skin of her back into red and purple mounds, and when he touched her there, she writhed towards him like a snake. But, he'll say he hadn't kissed her. He had not. It was, he'll say, as if kissing her would have started off a machinery within him, a process too complicated to explain. She rolled into him, tight. She couldn't, or wouldn't, see what she was doing to him. They were coming at this from different places, is what he'll say now. But what he remembers is hearing something, not so much a sound as a movement, coming from downstairs drifting upwards just then. He sensed it. No, he was aware of it. He tried to deny it, but she must have felt him hesitate, so seemed to try to make up for it by whispering something, and he remembers closing his eyes, overcome. Her breath was rotten when she turned her head, and their mouths were close in that excruciating moment that isn't a kiss, just yet. Not just yet. He remembers thinking, wondering what she would taste like. Not vanilla or cucumber, he knew that now, but like a new food he'd never tasted before? A certain type of raw vegetable, say, that he'd never tried but didn't know why, he just never had. Her hand, her fingers, he could feel them, begin to scribe circular patterns on his chest, his stomach, and down, and he felt himself tense, just in case she should be as scared as he was. In that light, to him, her flesh was as pale as butter, paler. But, he couldn't seem to lie still. It was like he was revving up to something he wouldn't have been able to control. Even so, there were sounds he heard, no, was aware of, outside the door. Through the wall, weak sounds of breath and footfalls. He pressed himself, his skin, to hers and drummed his fingers against her thigh. He could make out the sinews of her neck, pushed his lips into them and it felt, he'll say, like they, the two of them, had, just then, become an outcrop of each other. Already he was panicking, though, worried that she could feel the core of him, the metal of him, could hear it, the grind and click of him. And it was like something gave within him and the heat of his lips brushed her cheek, the corner of her mouth. And he lingered there, and he knew his breath was very thin. But light from under the door, violently fluorescent, spread like water across them both, and within the rectangle, a figure standing, only at first unsure. Gamble remembers this: he and Mara lying suddenly as still as cats. And at the door, an outline, an apparition, keys in hand, who seemed to take a moment to process the sight, who craned his neck in silhouetted interest, and who, without speaking, took a couple of paces into the room, as if he had a right, and who grabbed something from the window sill - a baseball cap. Even in that light, Gamble will say he could see the skin of the arm reach for the cap, and that the light caught the skin, and the skin was whiter than it should have been, whiter than powder, except for that line of blue script. He'll say it happened so fast, but he remembers hearing a snort, or a sniff, of a laugh, and there being a very slight hesitation, more through interest than surprise. And he remembers seeing the neck, the shoulders inflate, of there being a sense of movement - athletic, on the spot - and then the figure, the man, Gamble could see clearly by then, retreated away, like a cuckoo back into a clock, out into the hallway, and closed the door again.

Gamble says he fell slowly onto his back, away from Mara, placed the back of his hand on his forehead. Both he and she lay, he'll say, limp, quiet, exhausted. He'll say now, he was as sure as he could be of hearing laughter from the other side of the door.

Mara said. 'My boyfriend. He, sometimes, he lets himself in like that.'

Gamble's arm, he'll say, was caught beneath her and he slid it out and positioned it in the space between them. She turned, was looking at his profile. He was staring, towards the ceiling. He knew that she would be noticing, looking at, the little folds of skin under his chin like pleats of velvet. But it was as if he had reached his nadir. Heat from the fire burnished oddly green against the side of Mara's face, her shoulder. She altered the position of her legs. He'll say he was thankful that they had both been at least partly dressed - she still had her cheap panties on, and he had not even loosened the belt of his trousers.

He said, 'I'm sorry.' And he sat up.

'Don't be,' she said, and she sat up, too.

He looked at her only briefly then, and started fastening his shirt.

Her face was different, harder, he thought, hardened. Like a mix between a baby and a monster. He saw the shape of it receding, something ancient about the shadows under her eyes. He'll say, he knew he'd think about that later.

'I can't,' he said.

Even he will say he knew then that he was lying – not lying, exactly, just saying words, just putting a stop to things, putting a halt.

Mara waited, standing, by then, like a child being scolded.

He sighed, seemed to relax, she didn't even look three-di-mensional to him any more.

'I've only made one other mistake in my life,' he said, shaking his head. He'll say he wanted, needed to explain. 'I say "mistake". Jesus. Huge. Massive.'

He kept shaking his head like he was trying to delete a thought, he'll say.

'I'd like to say I fell for someone, but . . .' Talking about Hannah like that, he'll say, made it conspiratorial. He'll say now, he couldn't even begin to tell her what had happened.

But Gamble will say he felt like a door had been jimmied open and he was going to be forced to step inside. Either that, or it felt like something precious was tearing between them.

'But I do love her. Carolyn, I'm talking about now. My wife. But not, I don't know. Not . . .' He was struggling. It was like he was talking to himself. 'Not *fully*.'

He looked at her as if for support, and his eyes caught on the hooks of hers, and then it was like he was the scolded child, or the one in the confessional.

'It's more like, I don't know, like you'd feel about someone you've been in a room full of open doors with, you know? And the doors are slowly closing.'

He stood abruptly, and it startled Mara. She seemed to have to steady herself.

He felt fearsome, like an animal, he'll say now, but he can't quite place which type.

'But. Big "but".' He was pointing at her, Mara. Pointing. Jabbing his finger at her. 'We're a team, Carolyn and I. We still are. And I've lived like this – we have – for years now. And there's Isabelle, and there's . . .'

His voice began to sound fat, and he reached into his pocket for cigarettes, then lit one with a match. She must have been able to see his hands trembling.

'I don't know,' he said, in lazy smoke. 'I mean, I read somewhere that you can't replace dissatisfaction with desire. Some Buddhist shit, most likely.'

He drew thickly on the cigarette, and felt Mara watching him as the ash fell. He'll say he was amazed that she was still listening. And it was that: that she was still there, still listening. So he said, 'And life's short. And now there's you.' He'll say he tried to draw himself up to his full height as if he had suddenly found great strength. 'And there are some things I can't undo.'

He stepped forward, sure-footed, he hoped.

He'll say how he slid his hand through her hair at the back of her head, says doing it felt experimental, like he was learning, or re-learning. 'And I deserve you,' he said. He'd convinced himself.

He thought about kissing her, but he did not. Instead, he pulled her face to his shoulder. The smell of a struck match was between them.

'Let go now,' she'd said. He'll say he felt the words come out against him.

It's hard to explain - for Gamble to explain - why this should have felt so, what? Threatening? Those words were like a slow blade across his thigh, or his chest, and yet he'll say he just couldn't move away. Instead, he'll say he had a sense of watching himself falling, as if from a very tall building, of watching himself, arms outstretched, falling, but with a ridiculous mask of ecstasy on his face, of that body of his seeming to suddenly fly, seeming to ease itself onto the updraft, to soar for a moment, to rise on a thermal perhaps. And then, he'll say, and then, just as suddenly, to fall. And land. And burst open like a big, ripe fig.

'This is everything to me,' he remembers saying. 'Is this..?'

He'll say he wondered what kind of man he was, then. He'll say things were moving - more than just time - and he'll say now that he was hypnotised by it all, that he was in some sort of flow, thinking he could stop it, thinking he could stop himself, her, in just another minute, that he would not relapse. But her body looked different, naked. It seemed to have grown more substantial, to him. Her hair, he noticed her hair, it made her look like a wild thing, like a warrior. Something about her eyes didn't look real or right, though. The eyebrows faded into fans at the edges. And she carried herself differently, and there were patches of hair on her body - her armpits, her groin - so that she looked, to Gamble, like an abstract thing he couldn't quite get hold of. And so another minute went by and he still thought he could stop it. She wiped the back of her hand across her lips and her teeth, and it was like she was thinking, 'Yes. You've fallen for me already, haven't you? Of course you have.' It was like the tables were constantly turning. And when she kissed him, when she let him kiss her, it was eventual; not quite, but almost with demur. But he felt like he'd contracted her, and she held him like a – what? Like she was hungry, starving; like she was deprived. Fleetingly, he wondered what he might smell like to her: slight decay, or maybe mould, but he didn't retreat from her. He'll keep saying he thought he deserved her, that she was palliative. Close to, he saw her forehead, like a landscape of torn earth, he felt her hands, clenched, her arms, oddly cool.

He wanted to see what would happen, and he'll say he thought there was something beautifully repulsive about this vision of life teeming all over him. Even his soul felt liquid. Minutes worked themselves into longer and longer, and he thinks he forgot about trying to stop. Something like that. And he'll say now that the pain was part of it, part of some weird pleasure, and that, actually, it was like sleeping with someone made out of porcelain. But that didn't make it any the less gratifying.

And afterwards, they both smoked cigarette after cigarette and lay still. Mara was at first distant, and he feared he might have been insufficient, or worse, that she might have felt or sensed something fatal about him, and that made him want to please her, to be sure he had. He'll say, at that moment, he'd have done anything she asked of him, just to bring her back. He remembers looking at the clock on her bedside table; it was just gone seven but as dark as midnight even then. Then he looked back at Mara, lying stiller than water. He looked at her and saw the effort of calculation in the stillness of her.

'Are you okay?' he whispered, and thought about placing his hand on her chest, or his arm round her, but didn't, not just then.

Something vibrated in her throat, and he thought, at first, it was a sob, but it was so dark in that room, even sound was changed, and he wanted to want her again, but the feeling went, it was only like a twinge, and it went. He remembers moving his hand and placing it on her thigh. He thought she was going to push his hand away or turn over, or cry.

Just for a moment, uncertainty held him still. But, he'll say knew he had *deserved* her.

He'd watched the morning come. He'd stayed with her but hadn't slept all night. The bed had felt boiling hot, it was because of the feel of her skin, her body next to his, against his, her hip against his. He'd ached – his body had – and he'd needed to adjust himself, to move into a different position, but had been afraid of rousing her, of waking her, Mara, that is. Eventually, he'd had to creep out from next to her, to dip himself low, to hope the floorboards didn't creak and the door would just close quietly. He'll say now, that it wasn't that he felt guilty. Not at all. He just didn't want to wake her. She looked, he'll say, sinless, in sleep. The smell of her had still been all over him. Even when he dressed, he could still smell her. She'd made him want to shut the rest of the world out, close those blinds, leave the Black Country, start again. Nothing else mattered to him. Nothing. He was scared, yes, but actually, it was the purest of happinesses he was feeling. Despite everything, he felt purified. And that had shocked him. He couldn't get out from under the feelings she'd stirred in him. He felt different. He felt like, overnight, he'd slipped into another stage. He was tying his shoe laces just outside her bedroom door when he remembered the poem he'd copied out. The paper had remained folded in his trouser pocket but when he looked, the handwriting didn't look like his any more. He thought about leaving it, the poem, on the pillow beside her, next to her ear, but didn't. Instead, he left it on the mantelpiece above the gas fire, next to a gleam of dried wax from a candle. Somehow that seemed, he didn't know what exactly: better? Less twee? Less literal. Now, when he thinks back, he'll say he remembers only glancing at the jar, and the little packets of crushed pearls in there.

He was, of course, re-designing himself into something, or someone, the man, he thought he'd always wanted to be – the one he should have been. To him, then, Mara represented his fate, and he'd never realised he believed in all that, and he would have been fearful of that, naturally, the danger of it.

But somehow it was the *comfort* of danger that was pushing him on, he'll tell you now. It was filling him up. Once he was outside, though, the air there between his house and that building felt different to him, like it was mutating. It was a low bite of ash. He'd left the Old Doll Factory like he was leaving his only child on her first day at school, and he crossed the road trying not to look back. He was living inside his head, see. He wasn't actually *there*. He'll say he might have noticed a layer of frost on his car, and he'll say he might not have realised Carolyn's car wasn't even there, but still, he wasn't thinking straight. And inside his house, it felt chilly. The radiator in the hall was cold when he put his hand on it. Going round in his head was an excuse, a lie. He'd planned to say, if he'd been asked, that he'd slept downstairs or in the spare room, that he'd had a couple of glasses of wine and didn't want to disturb her, Carolyn. He doubted she'd even ask. But thinking back, he still can't explain why he felt the need to have to lie like that, to have to prepare a lie at all.

The kitchen, he'll tell you, was cold. It even smelt cold. There's a certain type of smell that empty houses have. It was like that: like a house that had lain empty for a while. He wondered if the boiler had broken and spent a couple of minutes just looking at it, scratching his head, looking for the flicker of blue flame through the little gap there. He flicked a switch and it fired up and he heard himself say, 'Ah,' like he'd just discovered an answer to a difficult question. He rubbed his hands together and shivered. He'll say he realised then he'd begun to always feel cold. He was aware that the house was very quiet but he was, he'll tell you now, hungry. And that was really all he could think about, being hungry. He opened the fridge and a gentle mist rolled out, or seemed to. But there was very little food in there, it seemed: an almost empty container of milk, which he shook, just to make sure, then opened and sniffed at, an out-of-date carton of margarine (because Carolyn insisted on butter and he'd inadvertently bought margarine that one time), a brown paper bag of dampish mushrooms, and an unopened pack of sliced ham. He sighed. His stomach grumbled, and he'll say he grabbed the pack of ham, peeled it open. The meat was thin, slithered with veins, so he stood, eating the ham, eating like he was starving, biting through the lines and veins. He ate slice after slice, slapping the food onto his tongue and sucking it in so that a whole slice rutted up against the top of his mouth, and, after he'd chewed it, bits of ham had to be twisted out with his little fingernail from between his teeth, before he would eat another slice. He'll say now it felt primeval, eating like that. It didn't matter to him that it was supermarket meat out of a vacuum pack with a barcode, he might as well have been eating a fresh kill. Which, he'll say now, made him think fleetingly of Hannah. And from that distance, just then, he didn't feel panic, or fear; not really, but he'll say now, he felt something, as dim as distant thunder and couldn't, quite, make out what it was exactly. He'll say he'd maybe thought it was the sound of Sunday church bells he could hear, or feel. He was thirsty, of course; eating all that ham had made him thirsty, and he opened a cupboard door or two, looking for glasses. It occurred to him that Carolyn must have tidied up, everything looked as though it had been put in a different place. This was, he thought, typical of Carolyn. It reminded him of how picky she was. He heard her voice in his head saying something about the importance of being organised, and of clearing up after yourself. He felt a clump of ham loosen between his back teeth, and remembers flicking it out with his tongue, spitting it onto his fingertip and looking at it. And he remembers placing it, this little bit of half chewed food, onto the worktop, and leaving it there. He found a glass, in the end, and drank water from it, a full pint, then wiped his mouth, his chin. Without washing it up, he left the glass next to the fragment of ham on the worktop. If you ask him what that was all about, he'll shake his head, lost for words. What he will say is that he felt suddenly overwhelmed with tiredness and he went to bed, his stomach full, his mind full, too. It was his intention to pack a few things, and, though he wasn't sure what would be next, he knew it wasn't what he had. And he sat, then lay on the bed in the spare room, only vaguely aware of hearing a particular sound, like when a car door's slammed, he thought, and really, he'll say he only intended to be quiet – to sit, or lie quietly – for a minute or two.

He must have fallen asleep straight away, though, and he seemed to have been placed, instantly, into a vivid, complicated dream in which he was watching, from afar, someone, a woman or a girl – he couldn't tell which – wading in a canal which wormed round and away into a distance. The water was at her hips and she seemed adrift, her back towards him, her shoulders bare. He was, he'll say, aware that this was a dream, that he was directing it himself, yet he'll say he didn't know, for sure, who the girl was, just that she was moving away from him, and that the only thing that stopped the whole scene feeling like it was from a powerful silent movie was that there seemed to be this accompaniment of thudding. Beside him, in this dream, was Carolyn, her face, an expression, cooled, and she was also looking towards the girl in the canal. In her hands, an unfolded paper which he recognised, or imagined to be the letter to him from the hospital. And though he tried to speak, to ask her or to explain to her, he couldn't seem to make the words come out, and so he looked back at the girl in the canal, and she was, by that time, deeper in the water, and her hair, which he wanted to be rapeseedy, not quite blonde, had lifted and was floating in longer and longer strands on the surface. He'd thought the thudding must have been coming from the girl, and though he could look *at* her, he was trying to look *into* her before she disappeared – he knew he was trying to do that. In a way, it had seemed to him that he was directing himself in the actions of the girl. Her fragile body was tangled up in all that vast barrenness, yet the concrete and crumbling factories reduced it all to just a clutter, a mess, and he'll say he seemed to have no desire to help her. And the clarity of that thought, and the fact of both he and Carolyn watching this girl, made the whole vision stunningly subjective and strikingly intimate. In his sleep-state, he told himself that he had, in every way, been horrible to her, Carolyn, he'd been terrible. A terrible husband. But there was a well of something inside him that made him want to say 'so what?' and to escape from that feeling. And there was something thumping then, something more than before, and he found he couldn't witness or manipulate anything more because the thumping vibrated through his chest and up into his head, and he was torn from his inner, to his outer, consciousness, and his eyes opened to a red dark he didn't at first recognise. He'll say at first he couldn't make out the shape of his legs, the bed, the furniture in the room. And fading into his hearing like a pathos, was a voice, through the bricks, and the intermittent thump of someone knocking. Through breathed-on glass from that room, he saw the police car parked, and the scattered dance-like steps of two officers, and the mouth of one as his name was called and called.

He drove to the hospital. It took ages to get there, like it always did. Traffic lights at Merry Hill were against him, set after set – how many are there? Three, is it? All of them on red. It was because of the complexity of the phases and cycles, he thought. And he wondered why the police car he was following wasn't using its blue light, didn't know if to feel heartened about that would be wrong. It's a hinterland round there, between Stourbridge and Dudley. There's something about the shut-down factories and the over-optimism of the shops that is, in any circumstance, intensely sad. And, of course, Gamble kept to the speed limit, what with following the police car all the way to the hospital so everything passed him by in slower motion, and it was like a zoetrope of corrugated metal and finished industry he kept catching in the very corner of his vision.

But the hospital is a monstrosity. It looks like a big, temporary building. It doesn't look safe. It didn't look safe to Gamble as he drove round the car park there, looking for a space. He was thinking, this place is always busy. Always. And he was sure he'd lose his car park ticket, even though he said to himself, as he did it, 'I'm putting the ticket in my wallet, here,' like he always did.

The police officers waited for him outside the main entrance, and they walked in together like they knew each other, like it was all so amenable. The lights inside were a shock, though, and he was led – he let them lead him – into a room marked 'Family Room' and was surprised when they left him there by himself. Doing that seemed to shut him off from everything else, including all noise, so it felt religious. He didn't want to sit down. He'll say he tried to, but rose to his feet every time, because, he'll say, he felt that you address someone differently if they're standing – you tell them things in a different way – and it felt like if he was going to be told something, he wanted to be standing. So he prowled about, reading posters on the wall for bereavement counselling, care homes, quitting smoking. Quitting smoking. He put his hand in his trouser pocket and realised he'd left his cigarettes on the bedside table in the spare room, that, in his rush to answer the door, he'd left everything behind, his phone, his glasses, everything. It was because he'd rushed out. To have been woken by that knocking and calling had frightened him, of course, and then to have seen the police officers standing there on his doorstep, and he'll admit to not really processing anything they'd been telling him. Something about Isabelle and the hospital, but even then, standing in that 'Family Room' he still wasn't sure what had gone on, and it felt like a joke. It did: family. He tried to put the situation into context, but all he could feel was darkness trembling beneath the surface of everything. He had an urge to examine himself, to unzip his fly there and then and check to see if there was any change, to feel if he had suddenly made a recovery. A nurse passed by without looking in, but he saw her, thought he recognised her as the one who'd taken his blood before, and he felt that dull ache again, in his groin, his lower back. He settled on just adjusting himself, letting his hand, his fingers ripple across his groin, his thigh, but his chest felt heavy. He'll say it felt like loose pearls in his throat, in his chest, in his lungs. It was like he needed to cough and cough and never stop coughing. The police officers, he thought when he peered out, looked like they were in fancy dress. They were talking to a doctor, young and important looking. When they saw him looking, they all motioned for him to come out in one synchronised movement. It would have been funny, he'll say, if it hadn't been so sincerely done.

When he approached them, he said, 'Where is she?' and one of the officers said, 'They're working on her.'

Gamble thought about that, even later on, the term 'working on', especially in connection with a human, and his daughter in particular. He felt suddenly affronted, said, 'What do you mean exactly? It's Isabelle you're talking about, not a machine.' And the officer looked down, shuffled his feet a bit.

'How, anyway?' Gamble said.

The other officer breathed in through his teeth like a car mechanic might. 'Drugs, we think,' he said. And Gamble will say there was a definite glint in his eye.

'She's fifteen,' Gamble said. 'Where's she getting drugs from? And anyway, she was grounded. How did she even get out?'

But by then, everyone was looking down, shuffling their feet and Gamble felt like a monster, like Fritzl, he'll say.

'She'll be alright though?' He said it to everyone, anyone. He threw the line out like he hoped to hook a response, any response. But there was none.

Close to, the doctor looked as young as Gamble had initially thought. Younger, maybe. She said, 'We're moving Isabelle to ITU.' And she started writing something in a floppy paper file she was having difficulty holding onto. 'We're going to keep her unconscious.'

Gamble thought, they all think I know what's happened here. It was, he'll say, like he'd walked in mid-way through a film or a play.

'I'm sorry,' he said. 'I don't, I mean, I'm not. I don't understand. Look, what's she done?'

The doctor reeled herself away. It might have been impatience, or boredom. She glanced at the police officers, then back at the file. To Gamble, she seemed incapable of making eye-contact.

'We're not.' She sniffed, which seemed strange, the noise of it. 'We're not, sure, precisely.'

There is an odd-shaped clock, large, on the wall there, and Gamble will say he was sure he heard a whole minute click past.

'Tox screen shows up cocaine at least,' the doctor said, and she was flicking through the file then. 'And alcohol, and maybe more . . . . Bad mix.'

One of the police officers stepped forward, eager, and

said, 'How she ended up in the canal, we don't know.'

'And,' the doctor said. 'We're not altogether sure about any lasting head injury, so . . .'

She looked not at him, but near him, he'll say. Did another minute click by? Gamble thinks it probably did. He said, 'So?' But nobody answered, as if there was no suggestion that he was even asking a question, and they took him - led him, again - to see her. She was in a room by herself, a side ward he heard someone call it. 'She's in a side ward,' someone said, and he thought about the word, couldn't help himself. There was one of those curtains hanging, half-drawn, around a bed. Isabelle lay, he'll say, looking awkward, ordinary, tall, lying flat like that, which surprised him. Her eyeliner was just grime, or something was, smudged down her cheeks. Her legs were visible, bare, mottled, not covered by the blanket. He wondered where her trousers were. Did the hospital take them, her jeans? He thought. He concentrated first on her earlobe, the little piercing there he could only just see. There was, he realised, no earring, and there was, he'll admit, something lovely about that, something fascinating, something unassuming. But what about the tubes? There was one that looked to be part of her, part of her nose, attached to her cheek with tape, which he wanted to pick off, concerned she might be allergic, like he was. There was one that seemed to be feeding a vein in the back of her hand from a drip. Others sprouted from under the blanket where her chest was, attached to a, what, a heart monitor? He looked at the lines on a screen nearby scribing lame, silent, uneven patterns. And back up to her face, her head, where there was a bandage obscuring one of her eyebrows. One of her eyelids was swollen blue-black, the other not quite closed, so he could see a slit of eye. He'll say he wondered if she could see, or if she was blind to it all. He wanted her eyelids to twitch, or something. But they were still. There was no movement there. If she was dreaming, he thought, it wasn't a bad one. She looked, to him, he'll say, more ungrounded than stunned. And it wasn't quiet. A machine, somewhere, made a sucking noise, or maybe a buzzing sound, like one of the printed circuits was shot, he'll say. He can't, quite, describe it. But it made him think of what might be going on in Isabelle's head.

There was a single seat, plastic, and he drew it up close to the bed and sat down. When he leaned forward, it creaked, the chair did, and he thought it might not be safe, so he shuffled carefully to the edge of it, leaned in towards her. Something, blood, he guessed, was still wet and it had done something to her hair. It really did give her a peculiar charm, like a seraph, say, or a particular mythical sea-creature. He watched her chest rise and fall, and saw how that affected the tubes, how they slithered against each other. And he thought about her chest – not in the same way as he'd thought about Mara's, or even Carolyn's – how she was a woman, really, and would have developed into being a woman. He leaned forward, placed his elbows on the mattress and Isabelle didn't so much as flinch. He looked at her, he observed her, examined her face, like someone looking for their own face in a family photograph. He'll tell how he felt himself beginning to crumble, like old bricks. He could feel it happening. And he took hold of her hand. He'll say it was as if he believed she could keep him steady. In his way, he'll say he thought there was something unstupefied about her, that, actually, holding her hand like that she felt unbroken, that her goodness, the goodness of her, had been fattened out by whatever had happened to her. He

174

looked at her arm, the skin of it, and though the flesh there was whiter than it could possibly be, whiter than frost, whiter than powder, he could make out a bruise, or a collection of little bruises, just beginning, in the crook of her arm, and a little pinprick, maybe two or three of them. He could see the way the veins stood out there, like thin blue wires under her flesh. He'll say seeing that was like an out-of-body experience for him, that he couldn't quite admit to himself that he might have been blind to any of that. And he was bracing himself against her, trying not to let anything of him seep through into her, through those injured walls of her. He held her hand between both of his like she was involved in some kind of religious experience he was having. But really, and he's honest about this, Mara had flown into his head – scampered, more like – as a mouse does into a house for the warmth, battering round and sticking to the sides. That thought, she, Mara, didn't belong there, he knew, but he couldn't catch it, or her, to get rid of it. He wanted to throw a coat over her and gently remove her, take her outside of himself. But he couldn't seem to. And from where he was, even with his eyes closed, he could hear Carolyn's voice, he could *feel* her footsteps. He braced himself against Isabelle, felt her thumbnail against his forehead. He could smell old smoke on her fingers, or his, he couldn't tell which. Carolyn, when she arrived in the room, the side ward, said, 'Oh, God.' That was all.

He opened his eyes slowly, saw that she was wearing a dress, thought she looked like she'd been out somewhere, and he'd wanted to mention it, but they were beyond that, mentioning things like that. And, anyway, Carolyn seemed to be sniffing at the air.

He watched her move towards the bed. She crept, really. It

was like he wasn't there. And he watched her touch Isabelle's face like she was touching something from an entirely different species, like she'd done on the day Isabelle was born. Except this time, the wonder wasn't the same as then. And to him, though Isabelle's body remained dead still, her face seemed to change, and he recognised himself in her, and as he did he'll say she seemed horribly perfect, and it felt like vertigo, and he heard himself breathing like there was no air in the room.

'Stop sighing like that,' Carolyn said, but without looking at him. 'You're always sighing.'

'I'm sorry,' he said, but he only said it because he thought speaking would keep him breathing.

Carolyn looked straight at him then. There were fibres of rain on her hair. Her eyes were brightened, but red-rimmed, and he couldn't tell if it was just because of the lighting in there. She'd clamped her lips together; there were remnants of dried lipstick along the edges. The feel of Isabelle's hand between his made him shiver, and he wanted to look anywhere but at her, or at Carolyn. So he looked at the wall, the dripstand, the metal of the bed, the little cupboard beside the bed, the plastic bag marked 'hospital property' on the little cupboard. He wanted to seem useful, practical, that was all. So he let go of her hand, and he opened the bag. Her jeans were there, some clothes, he could see them, touch them, and was aware of a smell – the canal, he thought, the water all over them – and he pulled them out of the bag, just for something to do that wasn't looking at Carolyn.

'What're you doing?' she said.

'I'm just,' he said, and he was searching for words. 'Checking. Seeing if, you know, all her stuff's in there.'

Carolyn's breathing was sharp little ticks. She said, 'What for? Your daughter's here. Look at her.'

He looked at her.

'No,' Carolyn said. '*Really* look at her.'

Gamble will say he felt under siege, like he wouldn't be able to do, to look, or behave correctly no matter how he did it.

'For Christ's sake,' Carolyn said. She was shouting. 'Are you blind, for fuck's sake?'

Gamble wanted to tell her to keep her voice down, he wanted to put his finger on his lips like he did at work when kids were getting lairy, but he was afraid of what she'd do. So he froze, like a cat held too tight, he absorbed the tension, he'll say. He fixed his look on Isabelle, her lips – perfect, even as she lay there like that – her still tongue. Every now and then, he'd been aware of a pain, a jabbing pain, which he imagined to be like the feel of broken glass under his skin across his groin and thighs, along his lower back. He guessed his face showed something, but hoped it didn't. Carolyn was silent for only a second and when she spoke, she seemed to have controlled her voice, tied it down like it might be blown away by gusts of anger if she didn't. She said, 'You never picked her up.' Gamble did look at her then, he said, 'What?'

'When she was little,' Carolyn said. 'You never once held her.'

Gamble said, 'Oh, I thought you meant . . .'

And the room was silent except for that sucking or buzzing or whatever it was.

'I thought I'd drop her,' Gamble said. 'I would have.'

He rubbed at the material of her clothes between his fingers. Sticky, he'll say.

'And, you know, I'm not . . . well, you know what I'm like.'

Carolyn, he noticed, glanced down at what he was holding. And her face changed. So that made him look: Isabelle's jeans, her underwear, between his fingers, yes, a T-shirt, also wet, tangled up and maybe torn so that it all looked like a conceptual experiment. And the smell, more soapy than anything else. For something to do, he'll say, he started to untangle, to unfold those clothes. He'll say he intended to put them back into the bag. But that's when he saw it. Inexplicable, at first, encroaching on her jeans, her clothes. He didn't realise what it was exactly straight away, because the first thing he saw was the emblem: an embroidered patch of an orchid, white - or had been - which he grabbed at, lifted, examined close-to. Of course, it was a baseball cap. The soap and scum of the canal clung to it.

'What's . . .' he said, and he held the cap by the brim, and it hung there, between him and Carolyn.

Carolyn was shaking her head. 'See. You didn't - you don't - know anything that's going on, do you?'

Gamble placed the cap on the bed. The embroidered orchid, he thought at first, looked phallic. And then Mara scuttled into his mind again, her face, her body. The smell of water, soap, whatever, was all over his hands and he didn't know where to put them. He ended up letting one hand settle on the zip of his trousers. It was for comfort, mainly.

'Clearly not,' he said.

He didn't want her to, not then, but it seemed that Carolyn took pity on him, or perhaps it was because of what she had to say.

'She had this . . .' She breathed in like a pronouncement was about to be made. 'This. Boyfriend.'

'Boyfriend?'

Isabelle lay stiller than death.

'I sort of knew about it.' Carolyn was scratching at her neck and little flakes of skin, or rain flimsied away. 'I mean, I knew there was someone. She sort of told me . . .' Her voice faded, or Gamble's hearing of it did. He picked the cap up.

'Christ,' he said.

'Yes, well.' Carolyn was flustered. 'I never actually met him.'

'Christ,' Gamble said, and he could feel himself receding. It was like a curtain coming down in front of his vision, he'll say, like a blind being dropped.

'Don't you dare get shitty.' Carolyn spoke through gritted teeth, her voice in danger of being flung up and away again. 'She's too much like you, Isabelle is. She thinks she can get away with things.'

The way she looked at him, the way she glared, that meant something, he was sure now. When he looked at Isabelle, it was like she knew the answer to everything.

He stood up, and the sudden heaviness he felt around his crotch made him stagger and he thought Carolyn would assume he'd been drinking.

'I'll go and get . . . things for her,' he said. 'From home.'

He kissed her, Isabelle, before he left. He'll say she tasted of nothing.

Whether Carolyn tried to stop him or not, he doesn't know, he'd stopped listening. And driving home, everything about the place seemed to close in, to gang up against him: all the empty factories, and the full ones, all the concrete and metal and bad air and weather, all of it seemed to know the answer to everything. And none of it looked familiar. Even when he pulled up outside his own house, nothing looked familiar to him. It was like, he'll say, something had clambered into his brain and had started destroying it. That it was all too late for him.

And, in Isabelle's room, he sat. Posters, on every wall, yes. Make-up and stationery. Magazines. He'll say he was thinking, who is this girl – my daughter – here? Who was she? He picked up a piece of paper from her bed. Isabelle had drawn, in blue ink, a design, a jumble of words scrawled downwards like a line of blue tattooed script. It was poetry, something he recognised, some misquote – he knew that straight away – from a Louise Bogan poem. *'Songs of the last act'* it said. He realised she must have been looking through his books, that she must have been in the spare room, looking through his things. He moved it – not exactly threw it – the piece of paper. And then he saw the envelope in amongst the rest of the bits of paper and pens and lipsticks, on her bed. It was the envelope addressed to him, the one from the hospital. It had been torn open and was empty, the letter had been removed. He skimmed his hand over the papers, the notepads, the rest of it, on her bed, suddenly wanting and not wanting to find the letter. Her bedside table was clear of all but perfumes, and he'll say he wondered if she'd put the letter in one of the drawers there, and that, if he looked, he'd find it. There was a waste-paper bin in the corner, and he thought about going through that, but didn't. Not then. And anyway, he'll say he already knew exactly what it would have said. He hadn't realised that from the window of her bedroom, it was possible see right out into the street. He'll say he lay down then, on Isabelle's bed. He ached, he'll say, everywhere. His head throbbed with it, and he'll say he was hoping that whatever it was that had clambered - scampered - into his brain would just reduce his worries.

He'll realise, soon, what the future holds, and it'll be, in a way, like a weight lifting, but he's not there yet, not quite. He'll say he just needed - needs - someone to talk to. Just to talk.

Which is probably why he keeps saying he likes to think she'll wait, that she'll hang on, that she expects him back, no matter what, that she won't let go. He must know nothing's certain, but he'll say they'll walk the towpath. And he listens, and he watches, and he's right, the water there is dark and flat, as only that water in Stourbridge Canal can be. It's alive though. And that's something.

Acknowledgements

I'D LIKE TO thank my Dad for his patience and interest, and for not being too horrified about the workings of my mind; my close family, for their encouragement; my daughter for promising to actually read the finished article; Chris and Jen Hamilton-Emery at Salt Publishing for agreeing to publish, and Nicholas Royle for his always excellent advice, his generosity and support, and his impeccable editing skills.

NEW FICTION FROM SALT

SAMUEL FISHER
The Chameleon (978-1-78463-124-6)

BEE LEWIS
Liminal (978-1-78463-138-3)

VESNA MAIN
Temptation: A User's Guide (978-1-78463-128-4)

ALISON MOORE
Missing (978-1-78463-140-6)

S.J. NAUDÉ
The Third Reel (978-1-78463-150-5)

HANNAH VINCENT
The Weaning (978-1-78463-120-8)

PHIL WHITAKER
You (978-1-78463-144-4)

This book has been typeset by
SALT PUBLISHING LIMITED
using Neacademia, a font designed by Sergei Egorov
for the Rosetta Type Foundry in the Czech Republic.
It is manufactured using Creamy 70gsm, a Forest
Stewardship Council™ certified paper from Stora Enso's
Anjala Mill in Finland. It was printed and bound by
Clays Limited in Bungay, Suffolk, Great Britain.

CROMER
GREAT BRITAIN
MMXVIII